Miami
PuritY

PANTHEON

BOOKS

NEW

YORK

Miami Purity

Vicki Hendricks

Library of Congress Cataloging-in-Publication Data

Hendricks, Vicki.
Miami purity / Vicki Hendricks.
p.   cm.
ISBN 0-679-43988-9
I. Title.
PS3558.E495187M53   1995
813'.54—dc20

Book design by Joanne Metsch

Manufactured in the United States of America
First Edition
2 4 6 8 9 7 5 3 1

For
Betty Owen,
Lynne Barrett,
my son, Ben Hendricks,
and my mom, Claire Robinson,
who encouraged me before she
knew what I was doing

Passions themselves are freedoms caught in their own trap.

—JEAN-PAUL SARTRE,
from *Sartre on Theater*

Miami
PuritY

one

HANK WAS DRUNK AND HE SLUGGED ME—IT WASN'T the first time—and I picked up the radio and caught him across the forehead with it. It was one of those big boom boxes with the cassette player and recorder, but I never figured it would kill him. We were sitting in front of the fan, listening to country music and sipping Jack Daniels—calling each other "Toots" like we both enjoyed—and all of a sudden the whole world changed. My old man was dead. I didn't feel like I had anything to do with it. I didn't make that choice.

I spent a few days in jail till the law decided I wasn't to blame. It was Hank's long record got me out. He was known to the cops. Afterwards I went on drinking and missing that son of a bitch like hell. There were several months

I don't know what I was doing. He had a terrible mean streak, but we were good together—specially when we got our clothes off.

At some point I woke up from a blackout and was in the hospital. I had vague memories of an asshole buying me drinks and him on top of me in a musty smelling car. There were flashes of fist and the sound of it against my jaw, but I wasn't sure whose fist it was—I could've been mixing up another time. The nurse told me I looked like I'd been kicked, beat up so bad I was lucky to be alive. I don't know why I believed her—about being lucky—but after they patched me up and dried me out for a while I was ready to give it a go. Really try to make myself a life, for the very first time. It was a big mistake.

That morning in North Miami Hank was almost gone from my memory, and so was the half pint of peppermint schnapps I used to carry in my shoulder bag.

I handed over the nine bucks I had on me to the cab driver—close to my last in the world—slid toward the door, opened it, and hopped out.

"You're a quarter short, lady," the cab driver said.

I just kept scooting on my way. Didn't have a choice.

"Hotty bitch," he hollered. He stretched across and banged the door shut. I think he was trying to catch my ass-end in it.

Hotty—I didn't know the word. I glanced back at him as I stepped up on the curb. He was pissed but there was nothing worth doing about it. I took a last drag and threw my cigarette on the concrete. The pavement was slick and clean from a morning downpour.

I'd been job hunting along Biscayne and on Dixie. There were stretches of gas stations, a couple pay-by-the-hour motels I was familiar with, and 7-11's and insurance agencies and such, alongside bars and strip clubs. I'd had the driver make five stops. Ran the meter up just a hair too far not even thinking of a tip. So I stuck my chin up a little and kept walking. Didn't flinch when he laid his patch of rubber.

I liked what he said—hotty. I was hot all right. At thirty-six-looking-thirty, I was determined to get myself out of the dark bars and into the daylight. I figured I could do something besides mix a drink and puppet my bleached peach around in a blacklight. 'Course, I'd made good money at it, but it was all spent as fast as it could make the transfer from garter to nose. And then the rest of it kept up Hank's habits. There were other men over the years too, as long as I remember—since about age twelve. They'd all cost me, just not quite so much as Hank. I made em happy and didn't ask nothing for keeps. Thought there was love in their hearts.

My last job was dancing at Bubbles. I didn't want to get back with that crowd. I'd taken my last hit in the mouth—or anywhere. I wasn't complaining, but I'd made up my mind Hank was gonna be my last mistake.

What I had was a small efficiency—rent due, a wild head of bleached blond hair, and a dancer's ass, still tight as could be. My nose was clean. All I needed was a regular day job. The "Help Wanted" in the window said this was as good a place as any.

I looked through the smeary glass walls and saw a rack packed with clean clothes that circled the store. The morning was overcast but the rose-tinted plastic shrouds glistened under the fluorescents. Yeah, it looked good.

I'd been in Miami for a couple years, but I'd missed it all. Living on a buzz, I couldn't say I ever stopped to take notice of the surroundings—except for being warm. I rarely saw the outside of a bar since I left Cleveland, much less stepped into the ocean or even sat in the sun. Now I was beginning to look around. If Cleveland was the armpit of the world then Miami must be the eyes, clear, blue sparkling eyes with plenty of promises. It was all there for me.

I grabbed the door handle with one hand, smoothed down my miniskirt with the other, and strolled on into the Miami-Purity Dry Cleaners.

I walked up to the counter to wait for the girl. She was busy with a customer. She hit three buttons and the whole long rack of clothes started to sway and travel. It fanned a breeze up my skirt. I said to myself, yeah, I'd like to give that rack a whirl.

The girl was young, but I had better pairs of what usually counts in the world. She was dark, sweet looking, but heavy. Cuban probably. I knew how it worked. If they'd hire her they'd take me.

The customer headed out and I stepped up.

"Is your boss around?" I asked. "I'm interested in applying for the job."

"The lady who hires you is not here right now, but I will find the manager." She stuck out her hand and I took it. "I'm Marisol."

"Sherri," I said.

She went off to the back.

It was just a second before he came stepping out from behind the partition ahead of the girl. I took a look at that baby face, and those Jagger lips, and I got hot. He was wearing the cleanest shirt I ever saw, with a smooth, soft neck coming out of the open collar. Some dark curls feathered up from his chest.

I wasn't expecting a dry cleaner to start my juices running. It was the mix of innocence and animal that did it. He was looking at me with his bright blue eyes, sweet as a baby's.

I could feel the weight shift to my heels and my left hip swing out. I wanted to feel his hands grab at my hips while I watched those lips work. It was the first time since Hank my body started to heat up and come alive on its own. It felt good, but I knew I ought to watch it.

"What can I do for you?"

"I'm interested in a position," I said. I parked my tits on the counter between my elbows and crooked a thumb under my shoulder strap to keep steady. Looked real straight into his blue eyes. "What kind of position is it?"

"You can fill out an application, but we were expecting to hire a retired person. It only pays minimum."

I didn't know if I could live on that, but those lips were sure convincing. It had already been a long morning.

"It's handy," I said. "I've done worse. I'd like to give it a try."

I had his attention and I spoke a little lower, kinda privately with him.

"I've been workin the bars all my life. Now I'm after a change. When I saw your place, I got a feeling. You know—like fate brought me here. I said to myself, I'll walk right in and get that job. I can do cleaning. That's something I'm good at."

I watched his face. Looked at the shiny gold cross hanging around his neck. I figured he was a Christian. I knew a lot of dancers that were Christians and I admired their good intentions. He was sizing me up and down.

"It was an impulse. I believe in fate, don't you?" I said.

"Yeah. Anyway, I can give you an application." He put out his hand salesman-style. He had long clean fingers, and a tan muscular forearm showed below the crisp rolled shirt sleeve. "I'm the manager. My name is Payne."

I couldn't resist. "Ouch," I said. I kept my lips rounded an extra second while I took the hand, and then smiled. "Mine's Sherise Parlay. Sherri, for short."

One corner of his mouth went up smirky-like. "Payne was my grandfather's name. We're Irish—Mahoney." He slid a sheet of paper across the scratched white counter. "Here," he said. "Fill it out. The owner will be here in a few minutes. You'll have to wait. I can't make that kind of decision."

I sat down on a plastic lawn chair against the side wall. I could see he was watching so I made a little show of crossing my legs under my short pink skirt and wiping the sweat off my neck. My body was jittery. My foot started to jiggle and I put both feet down flat on the floor. I knew I didn't have to fuck Payne to get the job, but I would've felt more comfortable with that.

The application was long and complicated, like most I filled out that morning. I wasn't sure if I did it right. I guessed at some dates. When I finished I gave it an overall glance. The page was printed neat but it showed up the blanks in my life. Well, I wouldn't lie. It was a fresh start. I could feel the bad luck dropping off my back making my shoulders lighter.

I sat still and straight, looking like I'd applied for regular day jobs a hundred times and gotten em.

"Here she comes," he said. I saw the woman before she flung open the glass door. Her lips said it all—those and her eyes, and thick dark hair—she matched him. She was his mother. She looked about ten years older than I was. Pretty good shape. Small and compact. Tough.

Payne introduced her as Brenda Mahoney.

She didn't waste time. "Let me see the application," she told him. Her face was kind of puffy up close, eyes yellowish with pink around the edges. Her hand was shaky when she held it out, and that tipped me off right away that she'd had a few too many the night before. Probably the night before that too, a long string of those nights. She started tapping the counter in front of her for him to slide the paperwork over there fast. He frowned and flung it to her like it burned.

I watched her face to see what she'd think when she got to my past employment, dancing and bar jobs with gaps in between where I couldn't recall or couldn't put down a name for what I was doing, but she didn't flinch.

"It's not a glamorous job," she said to me. "I'm not sure you'd like it."

I picked up the sweet scent of alcohol on her exhaled breath. She talked fast though, and didn't slur.

"You'll sweat in here, and your hair will frizz up. We can't use air conditioning because of all the steam—cold air would turn it into rain. And you have to be careful every second. You'll be using jets of steam for some fabrics and white-hot metal pressing plates on others."

I wondered how careful she was herself by afternoon if her drinking started this time in the morning.

She leaned forward and crossed her arms, fingering a gold cross with green stones that hung on a heavy chain between her tits. It was cute—mother and son both had their crosses. The stones were the color of her eyes that burned into me.

"If you touch one of those plates with your arm, the skin sears right to it."

"I'm real careful."

"Your past experience shows that you've always worked

with the public—in entertainment. You're in your thirties and never had a routine job. Are you sure you want this kind of responsibility?"

I nodded. "I'd appreciate it, Mrs. Mahoney. I'm ready to be responsible. I need the regular hours."

"Okay," she said and put her hands on her hips. "You sound like you mean it. Good. We've been trying to fill this position for a time now. I can see you have the energy, even if you lack the experience." She put a hand on my upper arm. I think she meant it to be firm and warm, but her nails were long and felt a little like claws.

"You'll eventually meet the other employees working their shifts on the pressers. We're all friends here." She moved her hand across for a shake. "Call me Brenda."

I looked at her face and thought, yes, maybe in ten years that's where I'll be—smart and tough, with the know-how to run my own business. "Thanks, Brenda," I said.

I glanced over the counter at Payne as she walked away. He looked fed up. His full lips were pursed and he was watching me with those cool blue eyes. I thought of grabbing the back of that thick curling dark hair and yanking his face down on mine.

"How about you?" I said. "Think I'll fit okay?"

He just looked at me and didn't say anything, but our eyes stuck for a second.

two

HEY STARTED ME THE NEXT DAY ON LAUNDERED
shirts. The shirts came out of the washer damp
and I had to rotate them through the three machines, one
that presses sleeves, one for collar and cuffs, and one for
the body. The body presser was a nice shapely torso, and I
could see the back side of the pants presser across the
room—an ass with legs. I knew it didn't have a boner in
front, but it gave me something to think about. I hadn't
had anybody but myself since Hank, that I remembered. I
was already horny as could be from looking at Payne in that
warm and steamy cleaners with the smell of fresh-washed
shirts making my breath catch. Reminded me of clean
men. I hadn't had many of those. Payne was one of the
sweetest I ever saw.

"Pretty good, for your first day."

With the churning of the industrial washer I hadn't heard him come up behind me. He checked the collar and looked over the shoulder at me.

"I don't expect you've done much ironing before." He looked at the perfect flat points I'd made on the bottom flaps.

"Not bad, hey?" I said.

"Yeah, pretty good, pretty good. You're learning." He looked down dreamy-like at the tails. "There's a dress shirt that comes in every week with a love note written in ink right here." He stroked the flap that tucks under the fly. "It says—let's see—it says—'These written words will remind you all day, of the love my lips will express tonight. XXX OOO, Me.'" He chuckled. "We could squirt some Jinx Ink on it and get it out, but it's the kind of thing that makes this joint bearable. I'll be sorry when that shirt is gone. Sometimes, on days when I feel stuck here, it's the only thing that reminds me life can be good."

I cocked my head and squinted up at him. I wasn't used to men telling their feelings around so easy. Hank sure didn't. Nobody did. I felt bad for Payne even if it didn't make sense. "What d'ya mean stuck?" I asked. "At your age you could do anything."

"Sure," he said.

"I understand about your mother being the boss. But overall there must be plenty of benefits."

"Yeah. Like a lot more money than I could make doing the same thing for anybody else. A lot more than I have time to spend."

"Yeah. That's my point. Most people'd give anything to be in your place. You're set up for life."

"Yeah, life. Like a prison sentence."

"I guess," I said, even though I didn't really see the problem. He had it good. I still wanted to kiss him and make it better—or whatever it took. I could do plenty to brighten up his life if he let me.

"Lately I've been thinkin about the future too," I said. "But it could be old age just pullin on my tits. Sometimes gravity just drags you down." I smiled so he got the joke and arched my tits up at him so he wouldn't get a mistaken notion that they were saggy. He took a look at the light nipple outlines that showed through my bra and blouse. For some reason his stare made me feel tacky. I crossed my arms. "Surely age couldn't be botherin you?" I asked. "How old are you?"

"Twenty-seven." He said it like he was ancient.

I looked at the smooth tan cheeks and full lips.

"Whew. Past your peak."

He smiled and I could see his white teeth. "You're making fun of me, but I feel like I've been here forever."

"Maybe you need some other interests. Got a girlfriend?"

"No. Not right now. I don't have a spare minute."

"Could be your problem right there. What do you do all the time?"

He stopped to think. "Paperwork mostly. Everything else that needs doing."

"How 'bout for fun?" I winked. "For sex? What do you do—jack off under the counter?"

His face got red and he put his knuckles against his hips. Too late I thought about this being a different kind of place from where I was used to. He wasn't one of the regulars from Bubbles who'd laugh and give me a pinch on the thigh for my wise-ass remark.

"Yeah, lady. And I do it in the boiler room, and in my office, sometimes right into some woman's silk pocket.

That's the best." He sniffed. "I don't think I like what comes out of your mouth."

"Sorry," I said. "I didn't mean anything. Really." I licked across my upper lip and took a chance. "I know how you can shut me up."

Before he could figure it out Brenda came walking over from her office on the left. "How's she doing?" she asked.

"Fine. She catches on fast." His lips formed the pout I'd noticed before.

"I'm learnin," I said.

I kept on with those shirts and by late afternoon I'd picked up some speed. I wasn't near the four hundred fifty that Payne said an experienced presser could do, but I finished the overnight service lots, and nobody would have to pick up my slack. That was important to me.

The work was hot, but like I said, I never minded the heat. And it was repetitious. My mind could drift. I let myself think of Hank for a while. It didn't hurt as much anymore. There was a sweetness attached to some of the drinking times we'd had together, the ones that weren't a haze. I remembered a birthday of mine that we'd spent at the bar down the street from our apartment.

Hank hardly ever brought me presents. None of my men were ever present-giving kinds of guys. Not that they wouldn't want to, they just couldn't organize enough to manage it. So I never expected Hank to pull a fat furry ball from under his shirt and plop it on the bar in my face. I felt my eyes sparkle up and I put both hands out to take it. It was slightly damp.

"You been sweatin on this thing all afternoon?" I asked him. I remember trying to keep my face from making a smile.

"C'mon. I just got it on my way here. A guy had em on

the hood of his car. This is the first time I heard you complain about gettin a wet pussy."

"Aren't you quick," I said. "I wasn't really complainin. It's the best present you ever gave me." I was running through the past couple years in my mind trying to think of what other presents he got for me.

"Toots, I think this is the only one," he said.

The fuzzy body was creamy tan except for a gray splotch on its chest and a brownish half-moon under its right eye. I held it up and saw it was a girl.

"Looks like you after I have to tone you down," Hank said.

I loved him for that. He was saying in his own way that he knew he got out of hand on me once in a while. It was the closest he ever came to a real sorry—when I didn't have a suitcase packed. Good enough for me. I got out of hand sometimes myself.

"It's already named Spot," he told me.

I kissed and cradled Spot like she was the kid me and Hank never had. The barmaid Jeannie got me a box and I kept the little puss next to my stool the rest of the night. Some of Hank's buddies were there and we all stayed late.

I lost track of what happened after a while, but in the morning when I woke up in bed, Spot was curled right between my legs. I touched Hank on the shoulder and when his eyes opened I pointed at the two blond pussies so comfortable together. He grunted and his eyes closed again, but he fell back asleep with half a smile.

The cat grew up real pretty in the next few months, but then one night I didn't make it home. Hank and me were in a fight. When we got back together a couple days later I didn't see Spot around. Hank said he gave her to a little kid in one of the apartments. She was getting too big.

I knew he did it cause I hurt him and I thought of trying to find her, but then I realized that she'd be better off in a home with a kid, and anyhow I couldn't take her back.

I visualized Hank so well, his teeth and eyes, every freckle on his arms, I sort of felt like he might turn up—he could walk right in the door of that cleaners if he wanted to and bring me another Spot. It seemed like he'd just left me, like all the times we left each other.

I was scheduled to work noon till nine, closing time that day, so it was part of my job to check supplies and set up for the next morning. That night Brenda took me to the front counter to show me how the lot numbers were used while Payne totaled the money in the cash register.

Brenda reached under the shelf after something and I looked over at Payne. "Thanks for being so patient with me today," I said. I grinned.

I saw him look to my left where Brenda was standing. I looked back at her and she was waiting for my attention, looking a little annoyed.

Her voice came out extra loud. "Everything is counted in lots of a hundred," she told me and held up a roll of tickets in bright colors. "And each lot has a different color, so we can see by what color we're on, how many hundred pieces we've run for the day. Then there's a separate sequence number so we can count how much business we do in a week and a month. You just have to be sure to set up the laundry and dry cleaning tickets in the right order." She pointed to each kind and placed them on the proper spools.

"Okay. Seems easy enough," I said.

"Most of our business is dependent on fast service, and the colored lots make it simple to count and locate items."

"Did you think of this all yourself?" I asked. She seemed

proud of her success and probably liked talking about it. Out of the corner of my eye I was watching Payne even up the piles of bills with his long fingers. I saw him tuck a twenty into his pants pocket.

"Not really. Most dry cleaners have something similar, as far as I know, but I started the extra sequential system that keeps a running total. That way we can estimate time and supplies easily. Our business varies according to the season, but I have a handle on it this way."

She turned to the rack and started smoothing down bags that weren't tucked up in the first place. I thought she was getting a little huffy. I wondered what the problem was. I hoped it wasn't me.

I heard Payne scooping out change and I looked over to see him caught up in rolling his quarters. I looked back at his mother. "I'm glad to see a woman can do so good on her own in business," I said.

She punched the buttons and her eyes flashed back light off the dancing plastic as the overhead rack whirled to zero. "I've got Payne to help me," she said. "But I'm due to open another store in less than two months. It's going to handle three times as much business as this one. Then Payne will take over here."

"That's really a high," I said. "I admire you. I'm even thinking I could follow your example. Maybe I could get a business of my own someday."

"Well, don't get carried away," she said. "It's hard work. You give up a major part of yourself—all your social life. You wouldn't want it."

I really thought I might. I wanted to give up a major part of myself. The part that kept getting me into trouble. If she could do it, so could I.

I took a glance at Payne again and he was finished at

the register. His eyes were headed in my direction, but I couldn't tell if he was staring at my tits or if his mind was on the moon. I told myself to cool it, but parts of me were heating up.

Brenda said she'd see him later and went on out back to her BMW.

"You all finished for the night?" I asked him.

"Just about. Sometimes I have a lot of paperwork to catch up, but lately it's been light for tourist season. Probably the rain."

"Got plans?"

"No. Just headed home. I'm pretty tired."

"Do you live with your mother?" I figured he did, but I wanted to see if he'd tell me.

"Right now, yes."

"Well, is she expecting you right away, or could you take me for something quick to eat?" I touched my stomach a little, my thumb grazed a tit. "I'm starved and near broke. Besides I'd like to talk to you."

"I'm short on cash," he said. "And my mother doesn't appreciate my dating the help. It's come up before."

"The help. Oh." I let my face show the hurt, but I should've expected that kind of answer.

"I'm sorry. I didn't mean it that way. I'm just out of practice talking to women socially."

"Hard to believe that," I said. "Okay, listen." I started to speak soft. "You can make it up to me, no problem. All you have to do is just drive, nothing else. We can pick up some Colonel Sanders and a six-pack, take it to my place. That twenty—the one you snitched—will more than cover it. I'll even pay you back on payday."

"I have to grab a few bucks like that," he said. "My mother keeps a tight hold on the cash. I'm expected to eat at home. But I can't complain; she buys me whatever I want."

"Just so I don't take the blame." I felt bad I'd said anything.

"Don't worry," he said, "I always fix the total."

"I wanna fix you," I said. Then I slowed down and heated up. I couldn't stop myself. "I've been sweating," I touched his neck at the collar, "and rubbing my thighs together—all afternoon." I unbuttoned his top button. "Looking at you, Payne. And I've seen you lookin right back."

I took my hand off his shirt and grazed across my tits. They were already pointed out hard under the silky shirt. Then I dipped my fingers down to the crotch of my jeans and pressed the thick seam so it pushed just right into the center of my bone. I could feel the heat flowing out of there.

He looked at me with his mouth open. His hand floated up—like by itself—and touched my nipple.

I was on him. I grabbed a handful of hair on the back of his head and forced those Jagger lips down hard against mine. He didn't resist. As soon as I got my mouth onto his, he forgot all about old Brenda. And those lips had muscles. I tested em with my teeth.

He popped the snap and yanked down my jeans and squeezed my ass strong enough to leave a full set of prints. I squeezed his and stuck my nails into his thin pants until he groaned. I ground my bone hard into him and I could feel him rock hard inside his pants. He pushed me off and boosted me onto the counter next to the rolls of quarters. I reached out to pull open his belt, but my elbow caught two rolls and knocked them off. They hit the concrete and burst loud in the empty building. Payne jumped back like he was woke from a trance. He glanced at me with my bare pussy aimed up at him and closed his eyes. His shoulders twitched.

I could feel my eyes wide open looking for an explanation but he didn't say a word and reached up a hand for me to straighten up and slide to my feet. I pulled at my jeans and wiggled my ass into them, all the time just staring at his blank face. My desire was clogged into a mad ball in my stomach so I bent down beside him and started to scoop up handfuls of quarters and pile them back on the counter. It gave me something to do while I wondered what was wrong with me—or him—or both of us—and kept me from talking snappy.

I knew our deal for the evening was off, so after we'd gotten the quarters all picked up I said goodnight. I left em for him to reroll.

"Sorry," he said. "I just noticed we were in plain view here with the lights on."

"Oh," I said. At least he was trying to make an excuse. "Well, we could go on to my place."

He motioned with his hands for me to stop or back off and shook his head. "I also remembered some business I have to take care of tonight. I really am sorry. I'll see you in the morning."

"Hey, no problem," I said. It seemed like pure fear had grabbed him by the balls, but I didn't have a clue of what I'd done to cause it. I turned and walked toward the office to pick up my bag and head out. I glanced back as I opened the door and he was bent over concentrating on rolling the quarters. I felt a little shaky inside. I couldn't remember ever getting a shove-off like that—except the time I puked on the guy's new shoes. I was a kid then. Hank sure never turned me down.

My stomach started to rumble from emptiness. I closed the door and stepped outside. "Fuck," I said. I hoped I still had one beer left in the refrigerator and at least half a box of spaghetti. I should've borrowed a fiver.

three

I WOKE UP THINKING I WASN'T GONNA SAY A WORD
to Payne unless he spoke to me first. I wasn't sure
if I could be friendly with somebody who just tromped
down on my feelings so fast and hard. I guess he hurt my
pussy-pride. He made me wonder for a second if I was really that scary. I thought he must have some deep trouble
inside to stand there with his bronco straining at the gate,
looking into a soft, wet, open invitation, and jolt backwards
like he was struck by lightning. But I knew he wasn't about
to tell me anything.

I didn't see him all morning and figured he would avoid
me the rest of the day, but he surprised me at the presser
after lunch. I was the only one back, so maybe he'd waited
in case of a scene.

"I felt bad last night," he said. "You didn't get any dinner." He looked at the toe of his right boot and then at me.

"I scraped up a little spaghetti," I said. "And today Marisol made me eat half the lunch her mother packed." I tapped my stomach. "I'll live."

"Well, I'd like to take you out tonight, if you're willing to try again."

The word no never came into my brain. It was easy to forgive him with his beautiful lips asking. "Sure," I said. "Let's just keep the same plan and forget about the false start."

That night after Brenda was gone and all the quarters were rolled, he led the way through the parking lot and opened the door of his black Corvette. I could feel the hot vibes coming off him. It was a total change from the night before and I didn't know or care why. He scooted into the driver's seat and right away nailed me with those lips. He had his tongue in my mouth and his hands in my hair and I could feel the heat waves rising and filling up the car. I was the one that broke it off. I was afraid he might freak again sitting there in the lot.

"Drive," I said. "Forget the Colonel and his chicken. Let's head to my apartment."

He put on the defroster to clear the steam and tromped the gas. We grabbed a twelve-pack at the 7-11 on the way.

As we stepped inside my place I felt a twinge and thought he might still bolt when his eyes adjusted to the decor—a secondhand mattress and an end table—but he only looked at me and dropped his shirt on the table and opened his belt.

I stopped mid-zipper on my own pants when I got a look at him. I felt my eyes bug and all the wind whoosh out of me. His cock was too big for his body, a regular column, a wonder of anti-gravity.

"Oh, my God," I said. I wondered if he even knew what he had there.

He finished pulling down his pants and then I collapsed on the mattress in front of him lolling in my own heat while he yanked my pants off and pulled my shirt over my head.

He knelt over me and guided his cock a little in and I felt myself already wet and coming from the tightness. He shoved harder and the smooth jab pushed me into the sunken mattress and he pinned my arms to the pillow and kept pounding. I was somewhere floating above him in my head. He dug in and stretched me out and I burned like I was a virgin. The vibrations moved up through my hips and chest right to my brain and I melted down. From then on I knew I was in trouble.

All night I kept crooning, "Payne, I'm feelin no pain." But I was joking. I felt every stroke. Next morning I was raw and swelled up. But, Jesus, I was feeling good. He was raw too, but we did it once more and his swelling finally went down.

He was quiet and looked up at the dark spots on the ceiling instead of at me while he was getting dressed. He picked up his pants and pulled out a side pocket to wipe his dick. I wanted to laugh thinking about him walking around all prissy clean at work with dried jism in his pocket.

"I got a bathroom you can wash up in. I don't mind a bit."

"No time," he said. "I've got to get into the shop and set up. He turned his pocket back inside and stepped into the pants. It was funny how perfect, clean and pressed, they looked. I'd be the only one to know what was in there. He must've invented a lot of tricks for looking clean and tidy all day at the shop.

"I'll have to listen to my mother's complaints about my

staying out all night. She likes me to call her every five minutes. I rarely go out, so she still worries. I'll be better off just seeing her at the shop. Cut the discussion short."

He said not to mention anything about us. Brenda might have a fit, and then I'd end up out of a job. He said she was kind of funny about sex anyway, since her divorce. The less she knew, the better. It was fine with me. I liked my job. I didn't want to get into it with Brenda.

When I got in, a little before noon, I could hear some mad goings-on in his office. She must've just come in. From the pitch I could tell it was hotter than steam in there.

"Just forget it. I'm not telling you!" he yelled. He was loud. "It's none of your goddamned business. You can't run my entire life."

"Oh yes. It is my business. And I don't think it's wise of you to forget it. My business. My fucking business."

I wondered how many times they had that same argument.

"Yeah," he said. He was quieter and I could just barely hear. "Don't I know that. I'm just your fucking puppet."

She must have said something else because there was a little wait and then she came slamming out. I ducked behind one of the pressers. With the whisker burn I had on my chin, I didn't want to meet up with her right then.

She swept by. She wasn't looking around. He must have kept my name out of it.

I wondered how long it was since Brenda had gotten laid. I guessed that was what she needed to round out her life, ease some of the pressure off Payne. But I couldn't think how I could help her.

For the rest of the day they acted even cooler than usual towards each other. Or hotter maybe with those looks that burn. I thought, shit, let the man have a life. You can't keep a healthy animal like that locked up. Fuck, I wanted him bad. Already I could feel something creeping through my stomach, making its way to my chest. It was kind of the same feeling I had for cocaine. I wasn't sure I could handle it either.

Now I see I should've just let it all alone, but I started to think about what I could do to change my luck. It was the pussy getting control over the head.

I spent several nights sitting home by myself. Payne said he really wanted to see me but he thought we should keep it cool for a while. He wanted to hang around the house and be a good boy. I was really antsy. I couldn't sleep.

I managed to sneak into his office to tease his parts a couple times when most of the other employees were out at break. We had trouble leaving each other alone if we got anywhere close by ourselves. The sneakiness of his slipping a finger in me or unbuttoning my shirt for a quick smooch made me all the hotter. I had the feel of him in me already, like I was used to getting it. I couldn't get enough. Doing it was the only thing that took my mind off wanting it, and a short time later the need would only be stronger.

Sexual heat was always permanent in me, no escaping it. I was hot for more ever since the first time—age twelve—so that's a lot of years. I traded rides on me for rides around the Red Mile back home in Lexington. I headed there on my bike almost every day till I was sixteen and left town. I can still smell that musky perfume of a horse's neck and hear the sound of their steamy snorts in the early morning. It was a good deal. Old Darrell gave me as many horse rides as I wanted. And I gave him plenty of horsing around.

I let him think he was getting what he shouldn't, but I

felt like I had it made at the time. He even let me train a little. Taught me to pick up each horse's rhythm, count the stride in thousands, know when to make it run full out. If I was a boy I probably could've become a jockey—no girl jockeys I knew of in those days. But then if I was a boy I doubt I'd have got those rides in the first place. 'Course I don't know for sure.

The sneaking around at work was mostly all Payne and me managed for a time, even though we were so hot together. He only came to my apartment once in that time. I stayed home the other nights making myself crazy, wondering if it was going to go on like that forever. I had to figure something out. He said he was smoothing things over with Brenda gradually, but I didn't know what to think. He didn't look like he was trying very hard to me. I was stuck on him to the point I could lose my head. That was a first. I couldn't remember ever losing my mind over a man, unless you count Hank after he was gone. That's why I had to keep pushing everything with Brenda, in order to get some relief.

I had break with her about a week after Payne's second visit. I was feeling jumpy.

"You work too hard," I told her.

She was dragging as we walked towards the back to put our sandwiches in the boiler room to heat up. The boiler was a monster-size metal drum that made steam for all the pressing machines. The heat in there would melt your cheese in a minute. We set the foil-wrapped sandwiches on the boiler and went outside the door to wait.

"What do you do to relax?" I asked her.

"Work some more," she said. "My business is my life now."

"Have a boyfriend?"

"I have no interest in getting remarried. Dating takes up time I don't have to spare."

It sounded like a prepared speech. I wondered if I could do anything to help her out. At least show her some fun. It would be good for both of us. It was my idea to loosen her up. Get her to like me so I could keep my job and be her son's lover. I needed more than I could get sneaking around. A finger a day wasn't going to keep me happy. I asked her if she'd want to go out for a drink some time.

"I might on an early night," she said. "It's been forever since I've gone out for fun. I'll let you know."

We grabbed our sandwiches. I had American cheese with pickles and when I bit into it the cheese was warm and tangy and reminded me of Payne. I thought that everything might work out for all of us.

four

BRENDA DIDN'T SAY ANYTHING, BUT MAYBE I START-ed her thinking. One night about a week later she didn't go home after closing. Payne gave me a call—I'd just got a phone—and said old mom was off getting plowed and he'd be out of there like lightning, heading over to see me. I didn't know how he could stand the sneaking around. It was like he was married to her.

I saw him drive up, so I had my clothes off when I open-ed the door. I'd bought a few things to fix the place up since the first time he was there. I had a radio tuned to some slinky jazz and my little lamp glowed rosy in the far corner behind me. I felt sexy standing in front of him showing my outline against the light.

I made my voice deep to reach out from the shadows. "Hi, baby," I said. "I'm all ready for ya."

I picked up his hand and sucked on his fingers and ran them down my tit and stomach and pushed one into the sweet spot that was oozing juice down my leg.

It didn't take him long to drop those fine pleated pants of his on the terrazzo floor. The thoroughbred was bucking inside the soft white cotton of his briefs. I snatched those down and shoved my face between his thighs and mashed my mouth against him and rubbed my cheeks in his pubic hair. He put his hands into my armpits and raised me up. He kicked those Fruit of the Looms, or whatever they were, into the corner. Neither one of us said a word and he gave me a push that dumped me into the mattress.

He climbed on top and I put a bite on that lower lip. We got a sweat worked up real fast. He had me lathered inside and out. He was all I could take, but I could take him over and over.

After he got his, he dozed off and I reached for the beer I had earlier. It was on the table under the driftwood lamp. I'd gotten the lamp at the thrift shop where I found the mattress and table earlier. I sipped my warm beer and looked at the smooth gray branches, bleached clean by the sun. I thought some guy might have picked up the wood on the beach and put in the electric himself.

I felt like I was on a vacation. Hadn't felt this peaceful ever. The memory of Hank was barely a tickle in the back of my brain. I picked up my cigarettes, lit one up, and sat there quiet. I noticed my lips sticking a little to the paper and the cool smoke filling up my chest. I was enjoying all the senses of my body, listening to Payne's soft breath in his sleep. I finished the beer and dropped the can into my new plastic wastebasket.

Payne woke up and I got us a couple more beers. We took turns massaging each other under the light. Everything sort of glowed. It was nice in there with the shininess of the terrazzo and the fresh white walls. I was thinking I might get some kind of a little palm tree to put by the window. I drew the shape of the palm I wanted on Payne's soft perfect back and made squiggly leaves that tickled him.

He laughed and turned over. Then I saw a bad burn on his thigh. He said he got it a few days before. I hadn't seen it because we didn't take his pants off at work that week—not even once. I touched around the edge of the redness real gentle.

"Baby, did it hurt?" I asked him. It was nearly in the pubic hair where it's so tender.

"Not that bad," he said. "I'm used to it. Forget it."

"How could you get used to that? How'd you manage to do it?" I took my finger and stroked lightly around the dark spot. He reached up and snapped the light off.

"I was trying to adjust one of the pants pressers and I leaned against the hot metal plate. It happens all the time in this business."

"I don't see how," I said. I tried to picture how he could twist himself and stick his groin against a leg presser, but it didn't seem possible. "I can't see it."

"Well, after you work here a while longer you will. I hope not, baby doll, but it's a hazard of the trade. You get burned in all kinds of unlikely places. You live with it." He pointed out the window. "Look, there's a full moon. See it? Look to the right when the wind blows that Christmas palm."

"It's pretty," I said. I looked at his face. It was smooth as a statue in the glow. "Not as pretty as you."

He gave me a long kiss with a lot of hot tongue in it and told me he loved me. It never sounded so good from anybody. I felt like he really meant it. Like I finally found the thing I'd always been after. Till that point I didn't even know what it was.

He lifted my hair and kissed me on the side of the neck and said he was going to try to see me more often. He wanted us to be together every night.

I could barely move my head to nod. I felt so heavy with love. I could feel it packed inside my chest. I didn't want to be even an arm's length away from him. He was so beautiful. I wanted to hold him and save him and make his whole world perfect. It was the first real purpose in life I ever had. Without a kid to raise, I'd only had to fill my own needs. My new dream was as huge and real as that glowing Miami moon. I hoped it wasn't so far away.

Payne said that in just a few months Brenda would open the new store and then she would be almost an hour's drive north. She would be dependent on him as a business partner and he could lay it on the line about us.

"I'll be the supervisor of this store and you'll become my manager," he told me. "I'll get an apartment on the beach for us."

"That's all I could want, babe. I never had anybody like you," I said. "My whole life feels fresh and pretty."

I couldn't even think about living on the beach. I couldn't imagine it. "Now you're really makin me nuts," I said. "I don't know if I can wait."

I told him about inviting his mother to go for a drink with me sometime. That it seemed natural she might get tired of doing her drinking alone at night.

"It's not a good idea at all," he said. "You'll just start her thinking. She's a suspicious person."

"I'm just sayin a casual drink. I can go easy."

"No. Listen. I don't want you to say anything more to her at all."

It was starting to get on my nerves the way he was questioning my judgment—like I didn't have sense enough to keep my mouth shut about us. "Trust me. I'm not an idiot," I said.

"Look. You get a few schnapps in you and you'll ruin both our lives. I don't want to hear another word. Subject closed."

"Give me a break," I said. "She puts away a hell of a lot more than I ever did. What's the harm in buyin her a few drinks? She might get to like me."

He glared at me. His face turned purplish red.

It wasn't till then I realized I'd gone too far and we were into a fight. But I was too mad to give in.

He put on his pants in a big hurry and grabbed his shirt off the floor. "If she hears a single word, has one suspicion, I will never touch you again."

"But—" My voice caught. I couldn't say a word to him. It was nuts. I went from feeling the best in my life to the worst. I couldn't understand it. I sat there with my arms empty and hanging.

"Payne, wait. Please."

He didn't even look at me. The full moon shone through the jalousies and shadows of palm fronds flashed across his back when he moved quick past the window. He slammed the door on his way out. I lit a cigarette and flopped back on the bed feeling numb, until I thought about his burn again. I could feel his pain inside of me. The question just hovered in my mind. How could he have burned himself through his pants like that without leaving a big singe mark?

The next day I felt miserable, and I could see he did too. I was sure I felt worse.

By noon I got really down. I was steaming dresses on lit-

tle Suzie—a contraption shaped like a woman in a skirt.
When you put a dress on her and hit the floor pedal, steam
billowed out, ballooning the dress and removing the wrinkles. We always laughed and made jokes about her huge
farts. Not this time. No sign of Payne. I couldn't unclench
my teeth. I was waiting for an apology—or at least some
explanation. I didn't have anything to say to him because I
couldn't see what I did wrong. I decided to sweat it out. I
waited all day and all night. I figured if he didn't want me
I was fucked. Nothing I could do. That night I drank a little schnapps—just one of those miniatures—but I didn't
cry. I thought that meant I was strong.

The next day I was doing inspections for the C.O.A.—
the Cover Our Ass list. I had to check for incoming holes,
burns, or permanent stains, and write everything down, in
case of false complaints. Brenda was off somewhere and
Payne came over and pretended to be checking up on my
work. He stuck his hand into a man's coat sleeve and
bowed like a magician. Then he pulled out a pair of black,
lacy, transparent panties. That quick he was all better.

I smiled but I could still feel the heaviness hanging on
my shoulders. I looked at his cheery face. I had to laugh.
"How'd you know those were in there?" I asked.

"I put them there," he whispered. "They're for you. We
find women's lingerie inside men's clothing a lot, but these
are new."

"You're so sneaky," I said. Then I whispered. "So where
are we now?"

"Miami-Purity."

"Stop it. I want to know if we're still lovers."

"Yes. Inseparable. Joined at the hips—sometimes other
places. You taught me a lesson."

"Oh, come on," I said. "Do you really love me?"

"Yep. I can't be without you. And you can talk to my mother if you're careful. Very careful. Just to get friendly."

He took me by the shoulders and stared into my face. "But you've got to be careful. And don't say anything about me that would show you're interested."

I looked at him and thought how crazy he was. I figured he really did love me, he seemed so happy. "Okay. I'll be careful. I don't want to ruin anything. I'm going to make friends is all. She might just lighten up."

"Don't count on it."

He glanced around and motioned me to his office. I followed fast and stepped inside. He unsnapped my jeans, yanked them down to my knees, and kissed my snatch almost before the door slammed shut. His erection pushed out the perfect pleats on the front of his trousers. He put all his strength into those lips when he kissed my mouth.

I took a breath. "A bird in the bush is worth two in the hand," I said. I was getting cheered up fast.

He opened his belt and zipper. I bent over the computer keyboard on his desk so he could poke me from behind. Yeah. He really loved me. I could feel his love deep inside. Yeah. Oh yeah. I was happy. I squeezed back with all the power of my soul.

We got into the pounding rhythm of the industrial-sized washer outside the door. Vom, vom, vom, vom, till it stopped and clanged into the spin cycle. Its shriek was barely louder than mine.

five

I MUST HAVE CAUGHT BRENDA ON A DAY WHEN SHE didn't get much of her usual, because she agreed easy to have a drink with me. She said she didn't have time to socialize, but she could have a drink once in a while on the way home. I figured she must be lonely. We might have a lot of stuff in common.

I took her down the street to Red Sky's Lounge. It was nice and cool and the lights were cut low. We slid onto some stools. The bartender gave us a wink and said, "How you girls tonight?" I figured he knew Brenda, but I was only familiar with the day crew. I'd been in there once or twice on break.

She said she was in the mood for a martini, so I ordered her a couple pretty quick to loosen her up. I told her I was really getting into my job now. I risked sounding silly and told her how I liked to watch the pretty pink bags swing around the rack and sparkle in the sun.

"They liven up all the clothes," I said. "Even brown and dark green glow inside that raspberry sherbet color."

"It's called 'Old Rose.' It's one of my favorite colors. I use a lot of it at home, all the towels, curtains, sheets. I never get tired of looking at it."

"It's feminine," I said. I thought, "pussy pink"—funny choice for such a tough old girl.

I got out a cigarette and looked up at the overhang and read the brass plaque for the umpteenth time. It was more interesting than watching the sweaty old men in golf shirts down the bar. Not much choice in that group.

"Red Sky's at night, Brenda, sailor's delight."

"This place isn't all that delightful," she said, "but it'll do." She raised her glass and looked at the plaque and sipped. "'Red sky at morning, sailor take warning.' The sky in Miami is red almost every morning—red bleeding into pink. Sort of a tie-dyed effect, very pretty. I used to get up to see it."

"I've seen it. Good thing we're not sailors." I laughed. I took a long draw on my cigarette and stuck my bottom lip out to blow the smoke to the ceiling. "You probably have to be a sailor to appreciate the decor." I motioned at the rumpled sail tacked across one wall trying to look decorative. "That thing needs a good cleaning."

She laughed and nodded. "That's what I was thinking."

I was starting to feel good, get comfortable with her. I stubbed out my cigarette in the middle of their anchor ashtray.

She was still looking around. "Not much going on in this place," she said. She held her drink in the direction of the old farts down the bar. "They need a stricter dress code in here."

I laughed. "We have some interesting stuff to look at in the shop. I like to check out the men's designer pants. Did you ever notice a nice pair of pants and think of what size—um—dick fits into them?"

She looked over at me. "Not really," she said.

Her face made me wonder if I'd gone too far. Surely she wasn't that much of a prude.

Then she sort of chuckled. "Is that what you're thinking when you steam the wrinkles out of the crotches?"

"Yeah. Sometimes. Clean clothes make me feel good—they look brand new again."

She was smiling and nodding almost sisterly at me so I kept on.

"Sometimes I get goose bumps when a man walks in to pick up his fresh laundered shirts—you know, the kind of guy with that soft perfect skin you wonder how he could grow a beard out of. He'll have on one of those shirts open in the front, still all crisp looking. I love the smooth tan neck coming up out of that white collar. Dark hair trimmed even across the back." I fanned at my neck. "It makes my knees weak." I took a swig of beer.

Her eyes opened up wider and I thought, oh shit, she knows who I'm talking about.

"Yeah?" she said. She started shaking her glass, making the olive roll around, but her voice stayed cool. "Is that what you think about while you're working?" Her leg was moving under the bar, like she couldn't sit still.

I reached down into my bag for another cigarette. "Not really. I concentrate on the job. I just notice when a guy looks good." I thought I'd change the subject. I took my time lighting up. "How long you been divorced?"

"Years," she said. She was still kind of glaring at me. It was another thing she didn't want to talk about.

I took a long draw on the cigarette. I knew I should drop the whole subject of men, but I couldn't give up that easy.

She was playing with her olive, dipping it into the martini and sucking off the juice, using her tongue to poke the pimiento back when it stuck out of the olive. Each time she took a sip she put her lips on the rim of the glass exactly on the lipstick blotch from before. The pink was thick on those smackers.

"Well, it must be nice to have a son around the house to keep you company."

"It is," she said.

"He date much?" I knew I couldn't get anywhere near putting my name together with his, so I was just fumbling. "He seems to work late a lot."

"He gets out plenty. He can't go out every night if he's going to keep up with the business. He's young, interested in his career getting started."

"Not too young to have fun," I said. I felt a little irritated at how she was pretending he had free time to go places, not to mention the money for it.

There was a pause. I wanted to say something, a hint that I knew he could hardly get out at all, but I'd already pushed too far. I thought about him having to swipe food money out of the cash register. It made me sick—with all she must have.

"He has plenty of time for that," she said. She bit into her olive while she looked at me.

I figured I better shut up. She started tapping her foot against the bar. I wondered how she could drink so much and still be so nervous.

She looked at her watch. "I'm going home for my swim."

"Tonight?" I said. I was thinking I hadn't gotten anywhere at all towards being her friend.

"I take a dip every night if it's not too rough. Keeps me in shape." She put a twenty on the bar and slung her bag over her shoulder.

"You get in the ocean after dark?"

"Sure. I've been doing it for years. I don't go out far."

"I stay out of the ocean, period," I said. "Ever since I saw *Jaws.*" I handed her back the twenty. "My treat."

I met Payne the next day in the big concrete room in back of the cleaners. It was a cool place with high ceilings so they could hang drapes to dry or be steamed. Other cleaners sent out the work, but Brenda had set it up to do all ours in the shop. That was her pride. More profit. The room made a nice place to meet, because the panels of drapes sectioned off pretty little private rooms and nobody had any business in there all day. We went to the farthest section to the back. I felt like I was in a fancy princess bed when I sat down on the floor and looked up into the layers of shiny red satin.

I took Payne's hand and pulled him down next to me and whispered that my talk with Brenda went okay. Maybe we would do it again some time. I'd taken it easy and stayed out of trouble with what I told her, but then I didn't manage to be her blood sister either. He didn't know what that was.

"You make a little cut," I told him, "either with a knife—or if you're chicken-shit you can stick your finger with a pin. Your friend does the same thing and then you put your wounds together and let your blood mix. Didn't you have a best friend when you were a kid? It's how you start a sacred bond."

"Sounds silly to me."

"Yeah. Kid stuff," I said. "There are better ways of makin sacred bonds."

I wrapped my body around him and held him by the back of the neck while I tilted my face to fit those lips and mashed them hard with a kiss and bit the lower one and tasted salty blood. He smeared those lips over my mouth and then he bit back. I felt the pain that comes with everything sacred.

The concrete was cool but hard, so I got him flat on his back with his hands behind his head. I held on to his biceps. I watched his slick dick move in and out while I squatted over him. I must've come three or four times real fast. My head went light and I felt the sweat running behind my knees. I was limber enough and he was long enough so I bent double and licked that sucker up and down a few times without it pulling out.

That really starched his collar. He couldn't hold on anymore and let out a loud groan. I hoped the presser in the back hadn't heard. Payne pushed me aside and was zipping up his pants before I caught my breath.

"We could be in trouble now," he said. He buttoned up, then flattened his pleats. "It's my fault. I shouldn't have let you get started."

"Take it easy," I whispered. I grabbed my jeans and started pulling the legs right side out. "The walls are concrete block. Nobody heard. Your mother's workin the steam cabinet up front. With all that hiss and vibration she can't hear a thing."

I tried to get him off the subject. He was looking so nervous. "I could use a steam cabinet like that at my place," I said. "Just stick my fancy blouses in there for a minute and they'd come out smooth as silk."

I put my feet through my pant's legs and lifted my hips to wiggle my ass in. A blood smear was on his chin and I dabbed it off with my finger and wiped it on my pants.

"You're crazy," he said. "That's a $3,000 machine. You don't need a $3,000 machine for the one fancy blouse you own. Bring it in."

"I was only kiddin," I said. "Just havin fun. I don't have a single fancy blouse. You don't need to get mean. What would I do with a thing like that?" I thought, Jesus, he's really touchy about this stuff. I'd pretty much thought he hated his work.

I had my clothes on by then and we came out of the curtains and walked toward the front. I scanned around for Brenda.

He pointed at the Chandler—the button-sewing machine—as we passed it. "That's one of our cheapest machines," he said, "and it costs several thousand. Each dry cleaning machine is $38,000. Then there's the reclaimer, and the pressers, and all the specialty machines. They're all my responsibility. Everything will belong to me some day."

"Okay. I'm impressed. But I'm not sure it's worth livin your life for," I said. "I've never had enough money to worry about the price of things, so I guess I don't understand the responsibility."

I sniffed. The smell of the dry cleaning fluid made my nose run. It would get to me every once in a while. "I'd rather spend my time worryin about you." I wanted to grab him around the neck and give him a long wet kiss to show him how bad I meant it, but I knew he wouldn't want to take the chance.

He went on toward the front. I stood there a second and watched his beautiful white neck and moved my eyes on down to watch the perfect soft fabric of his pants tighten with his steps. I licked the inside of my lip and tasted the salt of blood again. I wondered if it was his or mine.

The next day I was working up front with Marisol. We could watch Payne toward the back taking out some stains.

He was squirting on spotter and working it in real good with the "bone," a special tool shaped like a tongue depressor.

"What do you think?" I asked Marisol. I was in a mood for teasing. "Being a college girl, would you say that's a real bone?"

"Could be," she said, "but I think it is made of plastic."

"No, no. I mean the bone in Payne's pants."

I laughed. She giggled and covered her mouth.

"Don't talk about that—not with the hawk around."

"The hawk?"

"Brrrenda."

"She's a hawk? She looks more like a spoonbill to me. I saw a picture of one once in a bar, a funny old thing flappin across the Everglades. That beak—it was just like those pink lips."

"We call her 'hawk' because of the eye she keeps on Payne."

"I've noticed it."

"Brenda is always very fine to me—I am engaged." She held up a tiny diamond on her ring finger. "But another girl my same age, Katie, was here before you. Brenda did not like her. The girl had an accident. It was strange to me because I know she slept with Payne the night before."

"You sure?" I asked. I hadn't thought about him with a young girl. I didn't want to think about it.

"Yes, I am sure. A friend saw them together. The next day Brenda showed Katie how to take out rust with the hydrofluoric acid in the squeeze bottle—Brenda was drunk like usual, so maybe she didn't mean it—but the whole lid came off. Acid splashed all over the hand the girl used to hold the bone."

"How strong is that stuff?"

"It ate into her skin, burned deep." Marisol rubbed the back of her hand and looked at me. "Brenda helped her wash off right away, but it still burned bad. She cried. I took her to the doctor. They said she would keep the scar."

"Really think Brenda did it on purpose?"

"I do, yes. Everyone says she does not want Payne to have any girlfriend."

"Then the girl quit?"

"She never came in again. Brenda said she moved back up North."

A man walked up to the counter and handed me his ticket. I looked at the number and punched it into the computer box to bring his clothes around. I felt the cool breeze. I pulled out my collar and let the air fan my neck. A cream-color tie flew off and landed on my shoulder draping down my chest over my arm.

Marisol laughed. Her eyes got round. "It looks like the thing doctors put on to hold the arm," she said, "for a broken arm."

"A sling?"

"Yes, a sling." Then she frowned. "I think it could be a sign. Believe it—you better stay away from Payne."

"No Payne, no gain," I said. I tried to make it all a joke. I turned down my lower lip to look like Payne's and waggled the other hand in front of my crotch. Marisol giggled and I bent my wrist to make my fingers rise up together like a hard on. I laughed, but I didn't feel comical, only stupid.

Marisol stopped laughing and looked at me.

"I should take your advice," I said. I knew there wasn't a chance.

six

PULLED OUT MY PINT OF SCHNAPPS AND TOOK A swig. I was back on it, yeah, but only a little, under control. Surrounded by the eight-foot-high dry cleaning machines and reclaimer, nobody could see me and I didn't do it every day.

I was working the spotting board, trying to get out some blood. I squirted Streepro on the stain and worked it in. It was two months since I started at the cleaners. I'd learned every job in the place and they were all boring. I had Payne some nights, but never long enough. The hawk thought he was working out at the gym and he'd come over to my apartment instead. Then he'd go home and I'd smoke a couple joints for dinner in front of the nine-inch TV and try to keep calm. Nine inches of TV just wasn't enough.

I was starting to feel hopeless. Something was slipping away before I even knew what it meant to have it. I remembered the feeling. A year or so before the accident, Hank had nailed me good one night when I knew he shouldn't and I turned up pregnant for a second time in my life. I was never good at birth control if it took saying no.

"Go ahead and get rid of it," Hank said the day I told him. And I knew he was right, telling me straight out in his way that I was no June Cleaver or ever would be. I didn't need to think about it. I was no kind of a mother.

But then sadness—or maybe it was bad booze—snuck up on us that night. Hank never exactly said what he was feeling, but just on that one night I think we both felt that we had another kind of love in us that we'd never give a try. We whined and smeared ourselves on each other till we passed out—I guess. It was a sight I wouldn't want anybody to see. We were a sick couple of drunks, but maybe we were the closest we'd ever been—or else it was just the mix of booze and dope.

There were some complications and I went in the hospital. The doctor said I should get myself tied after that. I said, "You're the doc." I got the money and never mentioned it to Hank. He was on a binge. Then he was gone and I was empty of those kinds of worries, empty in general. But the evenings without Payne were worse emptiness.

A couple weeks earlier Payne had helped me get a driver's license and an old Chevy Impala with half a primer job to drive to work, but I didn't go sporting around town. It was too easy for me to get into trouble. I was keeping it cool for him but I wasn't a happy sight.

At night I'd started asking myself, so what am I doing here? Getting fucking nowhere with Payne was the answer. I wasn't even sure if he felt the same way about me as I did him. I could only wait so long for Brenda to move to the other store, for Payne and me to spend more time together. Ants were eating at my crotch. The old ants in the pants, it was a saying from my grandma.

I squirted the Streepro on again. I rubbed it in with the bone. I rubbed. I rubbed. I wasn't making any progress. The stain was deep into each thread. I couldn't stand it. This couldn't be how people lived. Every day was the same. I kept telling myself it's my job, I'll get used to it. I could stick with anything if I had Payne, but without him I was starting to feel like I'd rather be dead.

It's crap, I told myself. Maybe he doesn't even love me. Sitting around by myself so much was killing me. I decided if Payne didn't show up for his "workout" that night I would have to do something. I couldn't just sit there and rot. I'd go see some old friends. He was desperate to have me when he wanted, but he thought I'd always be there waiting.

I rubbed the spot so hard it marred the surface of the knit, but the stain was out. Worry about the hole later. What the hell? Anybody who'd send a golf shirt to the cleaners could afford to buy another one. I held it up and looked at it. The guy probably wouldn't notice.

That night at eight I took off for Bubbles 'n Jiggles, my old club. I couldn't sit home any longer. Payne was usually at my place by seven-thirty, if he was coming.

I could still find one or two friends at Bubbles and I'd limit my drinks to three. Just enough to relax.

It was a ten-minute drive in the heavy dusk traffic. The air conditioner in the car didn't work and the heat and fumes were strong. The lush tropical vegetation you saw on the Miami postcards couldn't quite suck the poison out of the air.

When I opened the door the bubble machine was working full force spewing out the sticky blobs right in my face. The soap scent was awful familiar, like some industrial stuff we used at the cleaners. I looked across the dark room toward the bar and thought—shit. My eyes weren't adjusted, and it was like a nightmare—dry cleaners in hell. In the dim glow the cigarette smoke swirled toward the ceiling like steam, and the outlines of torsos hovering in the blackness looked like hordes of pressing machines come to life. I was going nuts.

Then for a second I thought I saw Hank in his regular seat at the corner of the stage, in the spot where he was sitting the first time he tucked a dollar in my garter. I remembered the feel of his big rough-knuckled fingers. I didn't know if he was real loaded that night or just carried away, but at the end of my set when I was bare-ass he stood up and put his head into my thighs and I felt a hot wet path his tongue pushed between my pussy lips.

He was taking a real chance on getting a knee in the gut—or arrested if the cops would've been there. But I was a little high and got swept right away. It was like we were alone in the world. I held his face and stepped back finally, knowing I was already in trouble with the management. He stood there looking up at me with his mouth a little open and my wetness shining on his lips. The rest of the night he bought me one drink after another and our eyes never unlocked, till we got to his place and closed em and locked our other parts together.

I had to drag myself out of that memory. I was still standing in the doorway so I headed over to the bar and sat. The owner was working.

"Hi, babe, how's it going? It's been a while."

"Goin fine, Mike. Just fine. How about a double Jack." I

pointed a finger at the bottle. I figured I would just have two doubles, a single shot looked so skimpy in the glass.

"Sure. On the house for the old days." He snatched the bottle of Jack Daniels off the shelf and reached toward a glass. "No rocks tonight?"

"Yeah. I'll take my second one on the rocks." I winked. I dug into my bag and pulled out my cigarettes and fired one up. I picked up the squat glass he'd set on the bar, took about half the sweet liquid into my mouth, and swallowed. It burned a ways down. It felt nice. "I need to loosen up."

"Ol' Jack will do that for ya, babe. Now, seriously, are you in trouble? I've got a job for you if you need it."

"I don't think so."

He reached out and put his hand around my hand on the glass. "We miss you, you hear. We're your friends. Nobody blames you for what happened to Hank." He squeezed my hand. "I can give you a couple weekdays behind the bar and you can have Friday and Saturday nights to dance. You're still the best. You know it."

I just looked at him thinking how nice he was, and feeling sad I couldn't go back. Couldn't or wouldn't, it didn't matter.

He put his other hand on my shoulder. "Fucking forget what happened. It'd be good for you to come back to work."

I took his fingers off mine so I could lift the drink. "I know you're my friend. 'Preciate the offer. But I'm workin and doin fine. I got a job at a dry cleaners—a day job."

"Okay," he said. He looked like he didn't really believe it. "That's good. As long as it's what you want." He motioned toward the stage. "We haven't found anybody who can replace you though."

I glanced over. A girl I didn't know was shaking her tits

to the far side. She was young and pretty, but she didn't have any moves.

"I'm gettin too old to dance, Mike. You know it."

"Not you," he said. "I can see from here." He winked. "If I hadn't known you so long, I'd think you were in your twenties. You're still the best. Just say the word."

He got busy then. I took my drink and walked across the room to check out the new scenery. The nightmare feeling was gone now that I had my head on straight, and things looked cleaner and snazzier than I remembered. Maybe the walls were repainted. All three bubble machines were working and I'd never seen that before. It was magic the way the lights shimmered in the glassy balls.

I took a table and sat down with my Jack-rocks. A few bubbles floated past my face while I watched the girl on stage. She had a pink bead necklace stuck to her tits. It looked like it was hanging on the points of her nipples, but it didn't move when she bounced. She must've super-glued the plastic pearls to her skin to add a little class. She wasn't much of a dancer. The motions were jerky and she didn't have any range of movement, just squatted her bare pussy toward one face and then another.

Mike was right. I was still the best. I thought of getting up there and proving it with a couple of sliding splits. It was nice to be admired, gave me a kick. I could go back. Sure. Like hell. I was finished with the drugs and those kind of men. Playing games to stay alive. I had a real job. I just wanted more Payne—the good kind.

I looked back at the stage. She was sweet, but the young girls didn't take dancing seriously. Why should they? They made enough money. I could kiss one set of my lips with the other, but in that position—and most of the good ones—I had to wear the g-string by law. Men were more interested in the crack shots when a girl just squatted in front of their faces. I'd done it some too, pretending to cover my pussy lips with my fingers, but really splitting the lips a little to show some inside pink and let the aroma out to fetch some extra bucks later. Didn't take any special talent to do that. Easy money when you needed it.

But there were a few men who appreciated the graceful tough moves and toned muscles—Payne would, I bet, if he ever saw my routine. He'd never even been to a club. He was real shy about watching when I started moving to the music at my place.

Mike came towards my table with a glass. "Have one more on the house," he said. "I have to go. Don't forget about the job. It's waiting for ya."

"I won't forget, Mike." I swirled the Jack in my glass. "I'll keep sloshin the idea around. Thanks."

He laughed. "Okay. Take care."

There was no use thinking about it. Those Jagger lips won over any argument in my head. I turned to the bar and looked at the wide asses, pot bellies, and skinny rooster-claw necks. At least Hank wasn't there to spook me this time. Some choice. Worse than I remembered. And then you'd find out all the nastiness later. Take all the crap and do things you didn't want to. I knocked back my drink and sucked in a deep burning breath. I didn't need any part of that. I wanted my sweet Payne. I got out of there only a little over my limit.

seven

WOKE UP THE NEXT MORNING FEELING LIKE I made a giant mistake. I shouldn't've gone anywhere. What if Payne found out? I'd felt so caged up and lonesome I hadn't thought about his feelings, that he might think I went out to get some new stuff. Or some old stuff. Maybe I did and I was just lucky nobody turned up. Sometimes I felt like my mind wasn't working—or maybe my body was working overtime against it. I had to start thinking things through before it was too late. If it wasn't already.

I looked through the window at palm fronds against a blue sky and said to myself, hey, you could be living in Cleveland and looking at some gray shit right now. I had vivid memories of hunching my shoulders against that icy wind off the lake, nose frozen, legs stinging, enjoying the view of steel mill smokestacks while I fought my way to work. I'd let a man coax me up there—thinking with my clit. I had to thaw out my ass every night for a couple winters till I could get my shit in gear and head south. The only thing I missed from Cleveland was the beautiful, pure snow that covered up all the grime—you could see it if you got up early enough. I mostly remembered black slush.

I got to work a little early for the afternoon shift. Payne would be there in his office doing computer inventory. Brenda's car wasn't in the lot, so I decided to go straight in and see what the deal was.

I looked through the little window in his door. He was sitting there, his face toward the screen, his fingers slack on the computer keyboard. My stomach ground together and I knocked and walked in.

He turned toward me. His eyes were mean—solid red pig eyes. I figured he must've gone to my apartment.

"Good morning," I said. I tried for a perky sound to make everything seem okay.

"Yep, another day in paradise."

"Somethin the matter?"

"You can get your ass out of here."

"What do you mean?" I said. I already felt mad knowing I was gonna catch it and hadn't done nothing. "Are you kidding? What did I do?"

"Who didn't you do? That's the question, my dear. Last night—out fucking around. That's it for us, babe."

"No, I wasn't. I swear. I got sick of sittin around watchin TV, so I went out for a couple drinks is all. I didn't think you were comin over. I get lonesome there by myself wait-in. I feel like I'm goin nuts."

"I was the one waiting. I waited for three hours for you to come home. First I thought you went out to get something to eat. Then I worried you were in an accident. But I really knew what you were doing. I finally went home. I'm not the fool who's going to sit around waiting for you."

"I wasn't gone for three hours, no way. You must've come right after I left. And then it could've only been two hours max. Really, I just had a couple drinks. I thought you weren't comin over."

I heard Brenda's voice somewhere outside the office. She was giving Marisol orders about repressing some pants. Steam hissed out strong each time she pumped the floor pedal.

Payne heard her too. He knew he didn't have much time to grill me. "I don't believe a word you're saying," he said. "I know how you are, parading your tits and ass for every fat old man to gape at—and grab."

He took both my tits in his hands, shirt and all, and squeezed em hard together. "I bet you gave out a few feels, didn't you? For some free drinks. That's all you know how to do."

"You're wrong. Nobody touched me. And what if they looked? It doesn't hurt anybody."

"You're right at that. It damn well doesn't hurt me. You can just quit pretending that we have something together. You don't have the least idea what having a relationship means."

"I'll know it when I see it." I stopped. I didn't want to go any farther. "C'mon, baby. I've been a good girl. I love you. For the first time in my life, I'm behavin."

His pig eyes drilled into me, but he stayed quiet. The sound of Brenda's hacking cough came through the walls. I wanted a cigarette.

"There's no time to talk now. I'll finish what I have to say tonight—if you're home."

I knew I had him then. He couldn't give me up. The bad mood lifted off my head like a fog.

He didn't look at my face, just slid his hands under my shirt again and pinched my nipples flat between his fingers. Then he turned and walked off. I felt so good I went over to help Marisol steam some crotches before it was even time for me to start work.

That night I made a run to the Publix supermarket and picked up some beer, cheese, vegetables, and pepperoni. The pepperoni was for him cause I never ate animals since I was a kid. I'm always thinking how sweet those furry babies are. He liked when I made a plate of cold snacks, and we would sit around in the flicker of the little TV and play with each other. Once I'd let myself be the plate. A chunk of cheese on each nipple, a ripe olive on my belly button, pepperoni between the thighs. He said pepperoni went good with snatch.

"So what did you do last night?" he asked, while he was still coming in the door. The edge was off his anger, but he was trying to sound tough. All he really wanted to do was jump my ass.

"I told you, honey. I just had a couple drinks. That's it."

He wanted to know where. I told him. I said I would take him there sometime. He'd like seeing all the girls. We could bring one home and have a threesome. Right away I was sorry I said that. I pictured him plugging another dancer and I realized I didn't wanna share Payne for a night. He looked at me weird anyway. I kept forgetting how innocent he was. He was Catholic and had rules, and probably some guilt about sex. The whole world was good to him. He never had to grub for a meal or a bed. He was pure and beautiful.

"Did you dance?"

"No. I sure didn't. I don't work there anymore—unless I'm fired from the cleaners, I guess."

"Forget it. I didn't fire you. I was mad. Now I've decided to give you another chance. But there won't be any more chances."

"No way," I told him. "I won't need another chance." I dug my hand into his side pocket toward his groin and felt something big and hard. "Is that a role of silver dollars ya got there? Can I spend it?"

I looked into his eyes. They weren't piggish any more. "I just want yours, babe. Nobody else's. Nobody's like you."

He smiled and slid those lips over my mouth, and put his hands up under the T-shirt to graze my tits with his palms. He pulled the shirt off over my head and I rubbed my pussy against his hard-on under the pleats of soft cotton. I had this feeling like I wanted to crawl inside his body.

The next morning I woke up early and he was still there. Did that mean he was taking a stand against Brenda?

He rolled over to face me, still asleep, and I took my finger and traced around his eyes, then down his nose to his lips. Blub, blub. I flipped the lower lip out and let it smack back again. Blub. I wondered if my fooling with him was fitting in with some dream. I pulled down the soft bottom lip a little and looked at his teeth. Nice. Even. White. Clean down to the roots, like a colt, not like Hank's broken yellow ones. Payne was perfect, pure. I ran my fingertips down his smooth tan neck with the curling dark hair. He had a bite mark on the right side. I ought to watch what I'm doing, I thought. Looks sore. I didn't even remember biting him.

He opened his eyes, looked at me, and jumped out of bed. "Christ, I forgot to get up." He found his pants and started pulling them on, two legs at a time.

"Wait a sec," I said. "It's too late now anyway. Brenda knows you spent the night somewhere. You might as well be human and give me a kiss."

He blew out some air like I was asking for the moon and bent down to kiss my mouth.

"Now take it easy," I told him. "What about hittin her with the news about us?"

"No, I can't. Not yet. I'm sorry I have to tell you about this in such a hurry, but I didn't want to ruin last night with it."

"I don't wanna know."

He sat down next to me and kissed my forehead and tweaked my chin up. "The problem is we have a long wait until we can tell my mother about us. I'm sorry."

"Why? What do you mean?"

"There's a building code violation on the new place and it'll take months by the time it's fixed. The sprinkler system is bad. We need to have a new one installed."

"Fuck."

"Yeah. I don't know what to tell you. We're going to be stuck with my mother quite a while longer."

"Mother fuck," I said.

eight

I GOT TO WORK A LITTLE BEFORE NOON. MARISOL was up front tagging some cleaning, and the other pressers were busy mechanically shifting the clothes around, hitting the levers to lower the metal plates and pushing their floor pedals. The whole place was in a trance.

I walked past Payne's office and glanced through the little window. He wasn't there. I cut over to Brenda's. No Brenda. It was my day to handle laundered shirts, so I headed past the torsos to my station toward the back. It was three months since I started work and I'd learned enough in that time to be the fill-in person, moving around the shop to different jobs for everybody's sick days and days off. At least I got some variety that way.

I started pulling shirts from the bin where the first batch was waiting for me. Payne would've been there earlier to set the computerized washer. That was part of his morning routine.

I set up my first five shirts, each on a separate presser, and started rotating them through the machines. It was boring, but I'd gotten fast. It was to my credit with Brenda. I turned out to be much more of an asset than she'd expected.

"Hi, lover," Payne said. I was bent into the bin untangling some sleeves. He lifted the damp hair off the back of my neck and I felt the softness of those Jagger lips.

I raised up. "Shouldn't you watch it?"

"Everybody left for break except the girl at the desk. Brenda's gone off on errands. I've been sufficiently scolded for the day."

"Does she know where you were?"

"Of course not. You wouldn't be putting a shirt on the sleever right now if she did."

"It's a happy thought," I said. "I'm always this close to unemployment." I reached down and measured off a half inch with my fingers against his dick.

"Watch that," he said. He grabbed my hand and stuck it on my own crotch. "I told her I'd met a buddy at the spa and we got drunk and went from one bar to another all night. I passed out in the car. She can relate to that."

"She believed it?"

"I'm not sure. But why not?"

"What if she decides to boot you out of the business for misbehaving?"

"She won't. She's dependent enough on me. Now I just need the new store to open up so she'll be too busy with her own life to worry about mine."

I pressed a lever and steam billowed out between us. I

felt the heat getting to me. "That's never gonna happen. And I'm gettin sick of waiting. I'm fed up on ass kissin and swallowin words I want to spit out. You're just fine like you've always been, but I'm workin my pussy off for her and goin nowhere. And if she gets wind that you're pumpin me, I'm back at Bubbles, and you find yourself another chick."

I was on a roll. I glared up at him. "Face it. Brenda's not goin to leave you alone whether she opens that other store or not. No way we're ever gonna have more than a few fucks a week."

"Listen," he said. "I can't stand it either. I'm not going to let you go back to Bubbles or anywhere. We're going to stay together, even if I have to leave here and start my own business."

I didn't believe he'd do it for one second, but I could tell he believed it. "I don't know. That'd be crazy for you."

He was looking down, straightening the pleats in his pants. "I've never been on my own because I've never had a reason to be. My mother has always taken care of everything." He looked at me. "But now that we're together I can live without her and her money. I won't have to follow her orders. I'm so sick of the way she pushes me around."

I couldn't imagine Payne without his perfect-tailored designer pants and his black Corvette, but I was flattered he thought he could give it all up for me.

"I don't want to push you," I said. "Maybe we can take it easy for a while longer. You're worth the wait, honey."

"I'm trying to figure it all out. I don't want to fight with her and lose everything, but I have to do something real soon."

"So why'd you let her get away with it all this time? The bucks?"

"Yeah. And guilt. She told me a long time ago that I was

the reason my father left. He couldn't handle the responsibility. So I've tried to help her out, make up for him." He put a shaky hand up to touch my cheek and pushed a sweaty curl behind my ear. "But then I didn't have a reason to leave. Now I have. We can get out together."

Those were some of the best words I ever heard come from a guy's mouth. I took his hand and rolled it over my lips and kissed it, then squeezed it. I let go and he was putting his arm down when I saw a piece of gauze sticking out from his rolled sleeve. I pushed the sleeve up higher and looked at a rectangular bandage. It was fresh white against the dark thick hair on his forearm.

"What happened?"

"I bumped the Hoffman's," he said, "the hot metal plate on top."

I looked into his blue eyes. "Did Brenda do that to you?"

"That's an odd question." He tried to act casual, but I caught his eyes filling up.

I knew I better take it easy.

"It was an accident, that's all. I was tightening a loose bolt while she was having her fit about last night. I accidentally touched the hot part. That's all."

"I've never seen you cover a burn before."

"I just did it for an excuse to get out of her way. I went into the men's room and cooled it under water and bandaged it up."

"Let me see."

He knew I meant business so he held out his arm and I peeled back the adhesive tape, trying to do it slow and hold the hairs so they wouldn't pull. The mark was deep red with skin hanging loose in the middle. It was in the shape of a triangle, like the burn from a hand iron. The plate on the Hoffman's was square.

He looked up but didn't say anything. The tears started running down.

I held on to his arm and thought about all the burns he'd gotten since I'd known him. And one morning he had a split lip. Said he'd banged it. Then I remembered the bruise that I thought I gave him. I didn't. I was so stupid. I should've guessed. I just never heard of anything like that before—a woman purposely hurting her grown son.

He looked down at the toes of his ostrich skin boots. His lower lip was out a little, and his cheeks sucked in like he was gathering spit for a swallow, trying to think of something to say. Finally he looked back at me.

"It's okay, baby," I said. "We'll get out of here."

I heard the clank as the cycle changed on the dry cleaning machine. I watched the clothes tumbling round and round while he walked off toward the back.

nine

THAT NIGHT I SAT A LONG TIME ON THE FLOOR IN front of the TV, sucking down one beer after another. I smoked cigarettes and chewed my nails. I was lost trying to figure out what in hell was the matter with Brenda. Okay, women abused their kids and men abused their women—the ones with the strength used it. I couldn't figure where Brenda got the power to hurt Payne. To burn him, for Christ's sake. He could knock her on her ass and walk away. All that for the money?

I tried to remember conversations I'd heard between them. There weren't any—except the arguments that rumbled out from under closed office doors. Everything was family business. Like there was enough money and enough hate to overflow their lives if they weren't careful. It made them strained and awkward together. He'd jerk if she even brushed his arm.

I must've dozed off with my head back on the mattress, cause I woke up to loud knocking. A half-empty beer bottle was still in the hand on my lap. I set it on the floor and dragged myself up. I didn't know what time it was. I was wearing just a raggy T-shirt so I opened the door slow and peeked around.

The sight of Payne's smooth face perked me up like magic. I pulled him inside and wrapped my arms around his neck, crushed his face against mine. I took his head in my hands and moved his mouth toward me.

He was stiff at first. Then his tongue pushed inside my mouth and I felt his shoulders relax.

He pulled back. "She's disgusting tonight. Really tipped over. Started going over her long list of how much I owe her for the rest of my life. I couldn't stand to listen to it."

"I'm glad. Where'd you say you were goin?"

"For a drive."

"I was feelin real bad for you," I said. "I'm so happy you're here." I still felt sleepy and in a daze, and I drifted farther into it, tilting my head and kissing his neck, nipping with my lips, feeling a purr like a cat's in my throat. I opened the buttons on his shirt and rubbed my face down his chest, trying to get against as much warm skin as there was. He was leaning against the wall so I pulled him over to the bed and sat him down in the glow of the little lamp where I could see to work my way all over him. I slipped off his boots and raised his calves onto the bed. His legs felt extra heavy. His eyes were sad. He closed them and relaxed into the pillow.

I sat at his side and undid his belt and pants hook, pulled out his shirt, and nuzzled my face into his flat, tight stomach. He had a path of soft black hair that I followed downward, kissing, unzipping him an inch at a time, pulling his clean cotton underwear out of my way, sucking and licking. I rubbed my nose into him, snuffling like an animal. His cock was granite-hard under my hand where I held it against his hip. I licked closer to his thick pubic hair. He was making low sighs of pleasure. I raised up to watch as I pulled everything down to let it spring, that loveliest, smoothest, softest, hardest part of all.

Then I saw something. A thing I couldn't pass by. I strained to see closer, hoping I was mistaken. It was a smear of hot pink lipstick on the elastic edge of his underwear, above the "vin" in "Calvin Klein." I recognized the shade. I had my thumb a half inch from it and I froze and couldn't even move my eyes up to Payne's.

He must've seen the look on my face cause he sat up quick. He hesitated. "What's the matter?"

I couldn't say anything. I didn't have any air. I pointed. My finger was shaking.

"What? What's the matter?" He sat up and bent forward to see what I was looking at. "What is it?"

I knew he knew. His eyes were just as good as mine. I wasn't gonna say it.

"It's a stain or something," he said. He rubbed at it with his index finger and then the side of his hand. The smear widened. He paled.

I stared at him. He sat there with his lips clamped.

So this was the big secret he'd been holding onto, the reason his life was so tangled up in his mother.

I still couldn't get my breath. "Christ, you're fuckin her." I mouthed the words low. "You're doin us both."

He moved his head slowly, nodding the slightest bit. I could barely hear him speak. "More like she's fucking me."

"Christ," I hissed. "Jesus." I felt like my head would explode. I grabbed a handful of hair on the back of his neck and pulled his head closer to see his eyes. He had a glazed look, wide open innocent eyes. I felt so bad, and at the same time wild with anger. I pulled his head into my shoulder to try not to hurt him.

"Why didn't you tell me? Say you had all you needed? Jesus. You said you loved me. All this time you're fuckin us both." I felt the blood hot in my face, something red floating around us. I was sick for him. I pictured her lips on his cock, the thick look of her mouth. Pink smeared on his cock. Her ass gliding up and down on it in a room filled with perfume and sour pussy. I wanted to get my fingers around Brenda's throat.

I tightened my fist on his hair and pulled it harder. "How can you do it? Do her? How can you get hard for her?"

He didn't try to move, but I saw his face change. His neck went slack to the side. I let go of him.

"I don't know. I hate it. I don't know how to stop it. I try to keep her off me, but she begs, threatens. You can't possibly understand this."

I took a breath, held it a second before I let go, tried to keep from exploding. "I might. Tell me. Tell me how it started. Come on, cough it up before you gag on it."

"My father left when I was fifteen—"

"I never knew mine. Then he shot himself, so—" I stopped. "I'm sorry. Sorry."

He lifted his head and his eyes were blank. He looked back down. "It was bad for both of us. She started getting into bed with me at night to talk, and finally she'd pass out. One night she took her clothes off and touched me and took me into her mouth." A tear ran down his cheek and off his chin.

I felt bad, but my head was crazy. I couldn't say anything. I was thinking how many years he'd been doing her.

"It was my first time. I held still and didn't think. I didn't have much to do with it."

"And she's done it regular ever since?"

"No. Not regularly. Hardly ever. Only when she gets really smashed."

"Seems like every night to me."

"No. I mean it. Hardly ever. I don't dwell on it. It doesn't count. What can I do anyway?" He put on a flat smile. His eyes were sad and steady. "It's purely a physical manipulation. There's no kissing, no loving. Not like with us." He put his hand on my cheek, stroked my lips with his thumb.

His word "manipulation" made my throat tighten up. I kept seeing her doing it. "It means something," I said. "It sure means something." It meant one hell of a hold on him and a lot more I couldn't begin to figure out. I cut my eyes at him. "Do you want it, Payne?"

"No. I told you—I just can't stop it. I hate her. I feel sorry for her, and at the same time I hate her. I hate her so much I could almost kill her." He rubbed his hand hard across his eyes. "I don't know. I hate myself. I just have to keep from thinking about it."

I took his hand and held it. Somehow he could do his mother and not think about it. "You gotta leave. You're right. For us. And yourself. That's the only thing to do. You can't stay with her anymore. We can take off and head north—maybe to Sebastian, around there—get a little place and make a new life. Start over clean and fresh."

"Maybe," he said. "Maybe. But then—things might change when the new store is finished. I don't know." His face was blank, trancelike.

He's not gonna go, I thought. He's scared, making excuses.

He didn't look at me. He pulled his arm away and dropped it to his side, and I saw the burn again, skin scraped off a little in the center, raw. He was depending on the new store to change things. There wasn't a chance.

He stood up and hiked his pants and started to tuck his shirt in. I felt my stomach go hollow. He was resigned to his life. It made me think of my father again—what I'd heard. He lived a long time after he shot himself, eyeless, noseless, tongueless. Putting a shotgun under his chin should've finished him, but his head flew back. He never took another try, settled into a life with less than he ever had. He died slow of cancer years later.

Payne sat down on the mattress to pull his boots on. I watched the muscles in his back work. I didn't know what to do. I doubted if I could ever pry him out of there.

ten

I GOT ON WITH WORK THE NEXT MORNING, JUST like there was a blue sky up there, but I could only see the gray ceiling. It felt like it was dropping down on me. I felt cheated—I never had a chance. Maybe us having something, ever being together, was all in my wild imagination. He couldn't go with me. She had him so smothered and under control he couldn't even think. He was too young to figure anything out and he'd been too ashamed to tell. Probably felt like he was the only one in the world had ever done that. Every time I thought of it, heat poured off my body. I was hot as any metal plate.

Mechanically I rotated shirts through the machines. I started to hear the rhythm of her name in the grind the levers made when I pushed em. Bren-da . . . Bren-da . . . I tromped a steam pedal and I could hear it too. Brend . . . haa . . . Brend . . . haa . . . Brend . . . haa. . . .

It was a hiss from hell. I couldn't let go of it.

Payne stayed in his office all afternoon. I passed by every chance I got and watched him through the little window. I could see his back and his tapping fingers on the computer keyboard. He was into his routine. Maybe he felt safe like that. He didn't know anything else. If I didn't do something to keep him he'd just be done with me.

At five I saw him heading out the back toward his car and he hadn't said another word to me. A little later Brenda came up and told me he was sick. She asked if I'd work with her until closing that night, which meant after nine. It disgusted me to do her the favor, but I couldn't figure how to say no, or how to see Payne anyway, so I said okay and kept myself busy spotting stains in the back while she worked the desk. I had a break at seven and took my half-hour to run down the street to Red Sky's for a couple Jacks on the rocks. Why not? I didn't have much else to do.

When I got back I was loosened up and thinking how I'd just like to watch her face and tell her she had some great fucking taste in bed partners. But I didn't. I held back waiting to talk to Payne and hoping there was some way we could still be together. She went out for her break and I took over the desk. I stood right there and lit up a cigarette.

I'd bet money she went to Red Sky's same as me, cause when she got back she was weaving some wide curves. I watched her all the way to the front. She hit her arm against the steam cabinet and knocked the door open. That banged into her knee and she hung on it for a second before she closed it. I hadn't seen her this far gone before, but I'd never been around this late. Or maybe she was drinking extra over Payne, just like I was. When she got to me I saw her pants were open on the side. She must've stopped in the john.

"Where's Payne?" she said. "I need him right now. I need him to help me."

"You said he went home. You better sit down," I told her, "before you do some damage."

"Where's Payne? He needs to take care of his mom. Like a good son."

"Sit down, Brenda. Relax and get yourself together."

"What in hell are you talkin about?"

"You," I said. "The way you're lookin—like shit. I think you should go finish up in the back and let me take care of the last few customers. In about fifteen minutes I can total out the register and roll the change."

"You mus be kiddin," she said. "I'm not gonna take a chance on some cunt-wagger runnin off with my hard-earned money. You handle the back, and I'll finish up here." She picked up a pen and fumbled with the cap.

I started to walk and she called to me. "Hey, babe, better watch your mouth. Be your las night here."

Fuck her. I didn't say a word. She wouldn't remember any of it. I got to the back fast. I wanted to knock her wind out. But I could sympathize with a drunk—that's what saved her.

I had everything turned off and set up for the next day. The door was locked and I was running some schnapps around in my mouth to freshen up when she came stumbling back. She was holding a flask herself, so I took my time stowing the pint. She wasn't gonna remember it either.

She held her flask out like she was posing a toast. Then she swung it toward my head. I ducked and she lost her balance for a second and leaned against a machine.

"You're not so bad for a whore," she said. "To us." She coughed. "To us whores."

I pulled my schnapps back out and clinked glass against her metal. "To you," I said. I couldn't think what else to call her.

She must've slipped right then. Her legs flew straight out. She sat down hard on the concrete floor and banged her head against the dry cleaning machine. She bent forward stunned for a second, then leaned back and tilted her flask. I could hear her swallowing. It wouldn't've bothered me with anybody else, but watching Brenda made me want to puke.

I saw the lights were still blazing up front, so I left her sitting on her bruised ass and went to turn them out.

When I got there I saw that the quarters still needed to be rolled and put into the bag with the rest of the money. I wondered what to do about it—and her? I should've just left everything the way it was and took off, but I rolled the quarters and dropped em into the sack. There was a suit jacket all pressed and bagged in a clump on the floor, so I picked it up and punched its tag number into the computerized rack to bring the right slot to the front.

Even feeling lousy I still enjoyed watching those rosy bags of clothes sway and roll their way around the bend towards me. It was like a sideways ferris wheel. It started quick, got up speed, and then jerked to a stop. Round and round in whatever direction the button pusher made it go. Like my life, I thought. I start to think I'm getting somewhere but find out I'm really on the same old flat track going round.

I watched a tie sail out from the right rear, as usual, when it turned the curve. The rack came to a stop, and I hung the jacket where it belonged and clicked off the three sets of fluorescent lights. I could just see enough to walk back to Brenda by the glow of the emergency light in the back.

When I got to her she was passed out against the metal door of the machine. The tie that fell was looped in a funny way across her shoulder where her head lolled. Weird. She looked strangled. Like she was dead. She was out of it.

It made me think of Hank, how he must have looked all limp and pale, but I never remembered seeing him dead until the funeral. I imagined there was a lot of blood.

I stood there keeping my eye on Brenda and thinking about Hank and how easy it was for him to die and how unfair. I pulled a pink plastic bag off the bunch and looked at her pasty white face. She was out of this world, way far out. It seemed like a good place for her.

I bent down, slipped the plastic bag over her head, and stepped back. I don't know what made me do it. It seemed like such an easy thing to do. I stayed bent and stared at her face behind the pink film. She didn't move. I couldn't even tell if she was breathing.

I squatted and wrapped the tie firm around her neck, but not too tight, and made a bow. Her nose and lips were smashed flat, her bottom lip pulled down with teeth and gums showing. I felt queasy, but I kept picturing her face mashed against Payne's groin. I got up and searched the rack for another tie to hold her wrists. I stretched her arms to the leg of the spotting table and made a tight knot with the tie, even though I didn't expect her to wake up.

If she did, I don't know what I would've done, but she never moved a hair. I didn't really feel like I was hurting her. The cunt-pink plastic over her face gave her nice color. She'd suctioned it into her mouth and it looked like the inside of a little balloon.

After a few seconds I got nervous looking at her face so I rolled her head onto her chest. She didn't struggle. She didn't wake up. Just stayed there. I don't know how long I stood and stared at the top of her head. My shoulders jerked once like my arms wanted to do something to save her, but the rest of me held steady. I sat down in front of her.

At some point my hand went out and touched the plastic against her cheek. She felt dead. Cool and still. I started thinking I shouldn't've done it. I knew I shouldn't've. Fuck. I had to try something to save her.

I snagged the plastic and ripped it open down to her neck and loosened the tie. Her lipstick was smeared, but she looked okay. I'd seen her looking worse. I knelt down by her shoulder and untied her wrists and leaned over to see up close if she was breathing. I didn't think she was. I wondered if maybe I should give her a chance—try mouth-to-mouth. I'd seen pictures on the emergency card taped to the wall in her office. I didn't really know what I was doing, but I flattened her out on her back. I hoped I would wake up later and not remember anything.

I bent down and started to put my mouth against her lips. I touched her greasy pink lipstick and tasted rotten eggs coming up from her stomach, or maybe from mine. I jerked my head up and sat back on my heels. Physically I wanted her dead. Something inside me couldn't forgive her for those lips, what they did to Payne. It was my pussy started everything—sometime it had to stop.

I laid her head in my lap and untucked my shirt to wipe her lips. I rubbed the top lip clean and then the bottom. They were Payne's lips. She'd brought Payne into the world and she should live for that reason. She was just a victim of her own needs.

I put her head back on the floor, leaned over, and began to blow into her mouth. Some quick breaths and then a long slow one like I thought I remembered reading. The air didn't seem to be going in. I raised her head and tilted it more like the diagram and blew again. This time the air filled her chest and whistled back out through her mouth. It was sour and heavy with alcohol. I kept breathing into her, thinking of Payne, telling myself she didn't deserve to die. I don't know how long. It seemed long enough to make up for the damage I'd done, but it wasn't. I went on till I felt I'd given her my last breath. I looked at her face. It was bluish.

That was the way things wanted to go. She was past feeling any pain, maybe the best she ever felt. Could've been fate set it up and it wasn't for me to stop. I was there to save Payne. I might wake up later and not remember anything at all.

Then it hit me that I was in trouble. It didn't matter that I tried to revive her. I started to figure more clear. I got one of the big canvas laundry bags from a bin, the heavy-duty kind with a drawstring, to lug her outside. I put it around her ankles and bunched it up to make it slide on easy, like putting on pantyhose. The sooner I had the body in the bag, the less I'd have to see her and think about what I was doing. I hoisted her hips off the floor and tugged the bag up waist high. I tucked her arms down behind her into the sack.

I lifted her shoulders and pulled the canvas over her tits and up. The fucking bag was too short. I could only get it neck high and draw the cord. Her head was sticking out. I stared at her dark fringe of lashes and pouty mouth like Payne's, still sensuous. A chill crawled up my back. I shut my eyes.

Then I heard the rear door open. Christ. I was stunned. I knew it was Payne. He was the only one—besides Brenda—with a key. I heard him shut the door behind him and relock it. He flipped on the main switch that lit up most of the place again. He was fifty feet away, on the other side of the big machines.

I got up quick and ran to the back. I slowed up just as I rounded the last machine. He was walking straight toward me. "Hi, baby," I said. "Thought you were sick?"

"That's just the excuse I gave my mother. I had to get away from here—and her. But then I wondered if she'd be in good enough shape to close up. I was thinking—"

"Look. Let's go someplace else to talk. I don't wanna hang around here all night. Go check the boiler and make sure everything's set. I'll meet you back there in a second."

"Where's my mother? Isn't she here?"

I took a step back toward Brenda then turned around to answer him.

"She got sick too. I mean, she really got sick, puked her guts out. I told her to go on home and I'd take care of everything. You must have passed her on the way."

"Her car's still out back."

"She couldn't drive. You know how she gets. I called her a cab. Go on. Go on and check the boiler. Let's go."

"Yes, ma'am," he said. "All of a sudden there's another boss around here."

He turned on his heel toward the back.

I didn't say anything. I dashed around the machines to Brenda. Seeing her face again made my legs buckle. I grabbed onto a machine. I couldn't think. I figured I had to get her into it. Payne would want to check the front door alarm and he'd pass right by. I'd come back later when he was asleep and take her to the beach.

She was heavier than I thought, but I bent halfway inside the drum myself and managed to pull her in feet first under me, upside down. I grabbed her hair to lift her head up over the edge. I barely clicked the round glass door shut against the side of her face, when I heard Payne coming out of the boiler room. Then I remembered I needed her keys. She kept them on a hook in her office.

I snatched an out-of-order sign and stuck it over the glass with Brenda's face, so if Payne walked by he still wouldn't see her. I turned toward her office in the right front corner of the building.

He was heading toward me, almost even with the machine. "What are you doing?" he said. "Let's go."

"I have to get my purse from the office. Be right there."

"Okay. I'll check the front door."

I opened Brenda's office door and dashed inside. The keys were hanging in their place in a row of hooks behind the desk. I reached across for the one marked "Rear" and pulled it off the hook. A high-pitched animal wail—Payne's scream—made me jerk and drop the key and fall forward over the desk. The breath was gone out of me. I stayed there flat on my stomach.

Then I forced myself to go to Payne. I raised up and made it back into the main room. I could see him on his knees. He had the door of the machine open and his face flattened into the back of Brenda's neck with her head dangling out. The remains of the crumpled pink plastic sparkled like jewels in a pile on the floor underneath her black hair.

He didn't move when I walked over to him. He had his face down. His shoulders were shaking.

He looked up when I got next to him. His eyes were red and wet.

"You killed her," he said. I could barely hear him. "You fucking killed her."

He reached his hand right up my skirt and pulled down my panties. He grabbed my pussy, got a hold of the meat and dug his nails in. I didn't know if he was trying to hurt me or just get a grip. It hurt but it felt good. He had me under control and I didn't have to make any more decisions.

I looked down into his glassy eyes. "I didn't mean to kill her. I didn't mean to, Payne. I did, but I didn't. She was so drunk she couldn't stand up. I even tried to save her. I gave her mouth-to-mouth. I did, baby. Then I thought about how she hurt you all those years. I just wanted her to leave you alone so we could be together. I wanted you to have everything, and nobody to hurt you." I stroked his cheek. "She just passed out. Stopped breathin. She didn't have any happiness in life."

He raised his head up and stared at me. After a minute he shut his eyes. "It's true," he said. "But she's my mother." He looked back at her dangling head, bent down and rubbed his face in her hair.

"I tried to make you happy." He was talking to her. He lifted her hair in handfuls and let it spread out and fall. "I tried. I was the only one who ever tried. But it never worked. You wouldn't let me. I tried and I tried." He kept playing with her hair and stroking his fingertips over her cheeks.

Acid was burning in my stomach, but I kneeled down beside him and Brenda.

"She couldn't be happy," I said. "She was too far gone. She didn't know what was good for her—or you." I touched his hair, pushed it back. "It wasn't anybody's fault. It's the world." I kissed him on the forehead, then on his wet eyes. "I didn't mean to do it, not really."

He tilted his head against me. He was breathing hard and shaking.

"I can take care of you—much better than she did."

He touched her jaw and turned her face toward him, bent down to kiss her on the mouth. He was biting, biting down on her lip.

A noise came out of my throat and I took in a breath. He didn't hear. He didn't move. He didn't know I was there. I put my arms around his shoulders and my face against his head and held him as hard as I could. I was trying to squeeze her out of him. My arms tingled and I could feel heat pouring off my body. I wanted him to know I didn't mean to hurt him, that everything would be good for him from then on. He put his head down again on Brenda's neck and I squeezed them both. I buried my face alongside his in her thick black dead curls.

eleven

FTER A LONG TIME HE LIFTED HIS HEAD. HIS EYES were swollen and his nose was runny. Strands of her hair clung to his cheek like a web. I felt the same way he looked. Mascara stung my eyes. But his long wet lashes were beautiful.

We sat there for hours. I didn't know what else to do. I thought we would just stay there until the next day when somebody called the cops. It was crazy but while I was sitting there holding him I only just realized the odds against me. That I might have saved him for somebody else. I would probably go to prison—or the electric chair.

Finally he sat up and looked at me. His arms were down limp at his sides.

"I should kill you right now." He said it quiet. "Strangle you just like you did her."

"You're right," I said. "I wouldn't try to stop you. I've been thinkin about goin to jail and you being here, and some other woman would come along and take care of you. I couldn't stand it."

He looked at my neck and put both his hands around it, but lightly like a caress. Then he pulled my hair back hard with one hand. His eyes glared at me and he yanked my head to his shoulder.

"There's nothing I can do to change it," he said. "You did it. You killed her. You murdered my mother . . . and I still love you—and need you."

I grabbed his face in both hands then and mashed my mouth against those lips. He did love me. I knew it right then. I would love him—love him—love him—and love him some more. Never stop. I would be happy every day of my life just to touch his beautiful face. He couldn't get any woman better than me. Nobody could love him more than me or do more for him than I could. If I didn't have to go to the chair.

I stuck my tongue in his mouth and pulled him away from her onto the floor. I reached down and felt him—he was hard as ever. He wanted me too. We stripped down and did it right there, pounded it out fast, right next to his mother's dangling head. My foot touched her hair while I rode him.

When we were done, he lifted me off him and sat up. I felt warm and bleary.

"Okay. We're going to take care of this," he said. "Nobody's going to get caught."

I felt some better then. He was my partner. He was giving me my life, taking on the blame.

He stood up and pulled on his pants. "Cover her the rest of the way and let's get her out of here."

It was okay. I felt him getting under control. I straightened myself up and looked around. I pulled a soft angora sweater off the rack and slipped it over her head.

He stood there a second, biting his thumbnail.

"Okay, baby?" I asked him.

"Yeah, fine," he said. "Okay, grab an arm."

We grabbed at the sides of the bag for her arms and shoulders and pulled her the rest of the way out of the machine. Payne lifted her and put her down into a bin on wheels and dropped some fresh shirts on top of her. I threw away the plastic and we checked around the floor to see if anything was out of place. He found the empty flask and dropped it in the bin, then moved the out-of-order sign back to the broken machine. 'Course he knew where it belonged. I should've figured that would draw his attention right to her.

"Her purse," I said. I wheeled her to the back while he went to get her shoulder bag from the office. I pulled out my schnapps and finished the rest of it. Wished I had a little more. I lit up a cigarette.

It was around one o'clock in the morning when we got to their house on the beach. The body was in my trunk, but we still had to do something about her car.

We decided to get it out of sight before we finished with her. We rode back in Payne's Corvette. I opened the window and got some air. Cool breeze hit me in the face and blew my hair back. I felt the moisture on my skin, smelled the sea breeze. It was horrible what I did, but we were free. I looked over at him. He was staring frozen at the road. Me and Payne. She wasn't gonna hurt him again. We were tearing along to beat hell.

When we got back to the shop, I found some bobby pins in the bottom of my purse and pinned my hair down in a

twist on the back of my head the way Brenda did sometimes, until she got drunk and it all fell out. If anybody saw
me they wouldn't notice the blond hair so much. I could
probably pass for Brenda in the dark. Just old Brenda
swerving her way home in her BMW. Except I figured not
to swerve.

Payne said to keep to the neighborhood streets where
there weren't any bright lights. He showed me the headlights and how to start the car up. It was easy driving compared to my clunker.

It hit me that her car might be mine to drive someday.
Payne couldn't drive two cars. I didn't think about
Brenda's things before. What would happen to them? I
visualized my initials painted on the driver's side of the car,
like a dancer friend I used to know that got her own business going. Real classy. Mine would be S.I.P. with a flour-
ish—Sherri Isadora Parlay. My mother named me to be a
dancer, but she never knew I danced. At sixteen I left
Lexington to give up a kid. Ma gave up on me. I doubted
if she would've liked my kind of dancing. It kept me going
though, from Louisville to Cleveland to Miami. With dancing I never had to beg—but I was past that now.

S.I.P., a sip of Sherri. Sherri for sipping. Slow apprecia-
tion for the delicate flavor. Maybe with Payne I would be
delicate, have expensive taste. Jesus. It was sick to be thinking of what good I was going to have from killing her. It
didn't matter either. Just having Payne was what mattered.

He backed his car into the circular drive in front of the
Chevy and I parked behind it to block it from the street.
There were bushes along the front that covered the whole
right side and walls separating the yard from both neighbors. Somebody'd have to be going real slow to see anything.

Payne unlocked the trunk and I helped him lift her out.

He had the front door of the house open just a few feet away. He carried her by the armpits under the canvas bag, her head wrapped in the pink angora sweater hanging to the side, like when she was drunk. I held her under the thighs. I knew he could have carried her alone if I hadn't helped. He'd probably done it a lot.

He backed through the doorway and I shuffled in.

I felt a swish against my leg. "Jesus," I said. A big collie looked up at me from beside the door. "Christ, Payne, you never told me you had a dog."

"He won't hurt you."

The dog followed along next to Brenda. He was sniffing the sack at the spot where her pussy was.

"Go on. Beat it, Radar," Payne said.

"He's okay. He just scared me. How come he doesn't bark?"

"He's too interested. He usually does bark at strangers."

Payne hunched Brenda against his leg and reached over and pushed Radar's nose away. The dog backed off a little but kept following us.

I could see the moonlight coming in the glass sliding doors at the back of the house. We took Brenda straight through and lowered her to the tile in the kitchen. Payne stood there holding his head until I was getting near to panic.

Finally he put his hands down. "We'll have to get some salt water into her lungs if we're going to fake an accident, like she went for a swim drunk." He said he saw it on TV.

He told me to look around the house for a flexible tube, something thin that we could slide down her windpipe. He found a clean plastic milk jug and took it down to the surf to get some water. I thought of using a douche kit or enema tube and went to look in Brenda's bathroom.

I didn't know how plush they lived before. The room was

huge, with mirrors on two sides. It looked like a magazine picture. Everything matched the dark rose and peach tiles. The shower curtain had lace over rose, and the rose carpet was inches thick. There were extra faucets in the sink and they looked like solid gold. The closet was filled with big, thick, soft peach-colored towels with matching washcloths and little fringed towels embroidered with dark rose M's. It almost took my mind off why I was there, but not quite.

I bent over and looked in the cabinet under the sink. Sure enough, Brenda had douche and enema bags. I grabbed the stuff and took it to the kitchen.

Payne had the sweater off her head and the bag was pulled down to her feet. The tie I'd left around her neck was on the floor. He was stroking strands of hair away from her mouth.

All of a sudden I felt my knees go loose. Black spots started to float in front of my face. I tried to swallow, tried to make myself think. Seeing him touch her—even dead— made my stomach rise up. I sat down and put my head on his shoulder to get steady.

He took the hand from her face and tilted up my chin. "Let's get this thing down her throat and be done with it."

I picked up the pink hose from the douche bag and guided it between her lips. They were open just wide enough. Her head was back and her eyes were closed. Radar licked her ear.

I let the hose follow the bend down the back of her throat trying to be gentle—and hoped it went into her windpipe. Payne poured salt water into the rubber bulb, attached it to the hose, and gave it a few pumps—his last fuck with her. He pulled the tube out slow and then ran it back in again.

"Just to be safe," he said. His voice was shaky.

He pumped in water and pulled out the tube. He stood and grabbed her under the arms and I took a hold of her knees and lifted her legs to keep em from dragging. She still had her shoes on. She had all her clothes on.

"For Christ's sake, Payne, we gotta put on her bathing suit."

"She swims in the nude at night," he said. We set her back down on the tile. "We just have to undress her."

We squatted next to her and he started on the buttons down the front of her blouse. He was cool, all business. I unbuttoned the side of her pants. They were still unzipped. He pulled the shirt out and off her shoulders. She was wearing a black lace bra and her big brown nipples stared up at us.

He unhooked the front and pulled the cups back and dragged the straps off her arms along with the blouse. She sure had a pair. I pictured his mouth on them. His hand moved forward and I thought he was going to give her a last feel, but he didn't. He swallowed hard and sucked in a deep breath.

"Go ahead," he said. "Take off her pants. Let's get this done."

I slid the pants down her hips and yanked the black silk panties with them. Her thick curly black bush flashed out between bluish marbley thighs. I followed Payne's eyes down into the center of that devil's triangle.

"Okay," he said. "Pull those off. Hurry up."

I gave a last yank and the shoes came off inside the rest.

He stood and slid the door open. "I'm going to make sure none of the neighbors are taking a walk."

I sat down on a chair and watched him head out. I could follow his clothes for a while before he disappeared into the dark. It seemed a long time until I saw him coming back.

He stepped inside. "Let's go. It's clear. Get a hold under her knees."

I looked at him. He was wearing light tan pants and a white shirt. I had on a white shirt too. "Maybe we should take our clothes off," I said. "We'll be less easy to spot from down the beach. There's a piece of a moon."

"I don't know. Maybe. We don't need wet clothes lying around."

We pulled everything off and flung it all on a chair by the door, ready to put back on fast if we needed to.

I grabbed her knees and we moved outside and shuffled through the soft sand. She was heavy, just holding her legs under my arms. He was walking backwards and I was watching him and taking short steps. I could feel pieces like sticks and sharp shells under my feet, but it was too dark to see. We got to the firmer, wet sand and kept on going into the water. The soft crackly sound of foam swirling around my ankles was all I could hear.

"There aren't any waves tonight," I said. "How could she drown?"

"It's okay. It's perfect. No waves to bring her in, and the tide's going out. This is just the kind of night for her to take a long swim." He looked up at the sky. "With that crescent moon and all, I can nearly believe it myself. And she was plenty drunk this afternoon. People at the shop had to notice."

We lowered Brenda and guided her under the surface. I had her by the calves and was trudging through warm water that lapped at my pussy. I looked across her and watched Payne bent forward, stepping careful-like with the ocean above his knees. Even in that worst time of fear, I let my eyes slip up his body. I thought how beautiful he was, like a statue in the glow of moonlight. I wanted to feel his hands on me and slide my skin against him till I died.

Seaweed and slimy creatures grazed my ankle and I looked down. All I could see was the surface with light scattering around our floating shadows.

I stopped. "Let's do believe it," I said.

Payne took his eyes off Brenda and looked at me.

"Let's make ourselves believe it. It could've happened. From now on—she drowned, just like you said. I believe it, Payne. She would've drowned herself without us—without me—sooner or later. It's the truth and we can be happy."

"You're right. Once we let her go, it's all up to nature. She'll drift on down and disappear."

"She passed out cold. It was fate."

We walked her out until I was neck deep and then we let her go. She slipped below the surface easy, just like he said, those two headlights floating, staring up at us before she rolled and sank. Her white back shined a split second in the moonlight under that black velvet layer of water, like some huge, slow-moving fish, hiding with all the rest of the scavengers down there.

twelve

T TOOK A LONG TIME TO CLEAN UP AND CHECK ALL the details that night.

I felt sad and desperate and filled with hopes I didn't deserve to come true. But whatever happened to me, at least I'd saved Payne from Brenda's viciousness. If he didn't know it right then, I thought he would someday.

We never talked again about what really happened. She drowned. We didn't know anything. He said he would phone the police in the morning when he got up and saw his mother wasn't in her bed. He would tell em he went to bed early, sick. It would look like a regular day—except in my mind where there was a hulking, bloated fish, bumping along the rippled sand toward the beach.

I wanted to fuck Payne bad that night, fuck and fuck.

My blood was like electric under the skin and I knew fucking was the only thing that could settle it down. But he wouldn't touch me. I understood, but it was hell. He fell asleep and I was sure I'd never be able to sleep again. I couldn't even have a drink since there wasn't any in the house, or else Brenda had it hid.

My feelings kept changing. One time I even had the phone in my hand, starting to dial the cops—to give myself up. Payne must've heard the little clicks of the buttons in his sleep. He rolled next to me and put his arm around my waist and tucked his head under my arm. His cheek rested warm against my tit. I figured that was a sign. I'd done what I was meant to, for him. I set the phone back on the night table. For the rest of the night he slept and I watched him.

I left before dawn to go back to my place. Nobody saw me. When I got to work at noon I expected the police to be there. They weren't. Payne was in his office, crisp as usual, tapping on the computer. He looked fine.

"How are you, babe?" I asked him.

"I'm worried," he said. His eyebrows drew together. "My mother wasn't in her bed this morning. The door to her room was open. She hadn't slept there. Her car is in front of our house, but I didn't see her come home last night— I was in bed sick. I know she was drinking yesterday, a lot."

"She might have walked off and passed out on the beach somewhere," I said. "Or spent the night with somebody."

"I thought that earlier, but it's too late now. She would never miss a morning of work. I called the police."

I told him she could take care of herself, that maybe she had a hot date. "There's a first time for everything," I said.

"The cops think so too," he said. He was tapping his fingers nervously on the desk. "But they're looking. No sign of her so far."

"I'll keep you company tonight, make you feel better."

He grabbed me and held on tight, stuck his tongue in my mouth. I sucked on it good. Suddenly he pulled back. "You'd better not come over the first night," he said.

"Okay. It makes sense to wait a little."

I went out to start the laundered shirts. Any minute I expected Brenda to come marching in and complain about a collar not ironed right. Yeah, keep thinking like that, I told myself. It'll keep you in line. I pulled down the handles on the presser and looked over my shoulder.

The next couple weeks were the same. Brenda didn't turn up. Payne convinced me to keep to myself at the apartment for a while. "Until I get some word," he told me, "and see how it goes." He was afraid to give me his phone number because he said I would start calling and we couldn't take the chance of some kind of wiretap. He was being sensible. He called me a few times from the gym, and we talked about everything but Brenda. Each morning in his office we checked the *Herald* for news but never said out loud what we were after.

He had to talk to the cops a lot, but they seemed to believe his story. All the employees enjoyed telling them about Brenda's drinking. The cops asked me if I knew anybody that Brenda was seeing, or knew anything a woman might keep quiet about to her son. I told them she was a regular at the bar down the street. I'd been there with her once. I said she didn't have anybody in particular, not that I knew of.

They told me I was the last person to see her. I said I wasn't a real good friend, just an employee. I answered all their questions about my evening without any trouble. They didn't seem to be much worried about what I was doing. Since me and Payne always had to sneak to see each other, nobody knew I had a personal connection with the family.

I was worried about what they'd say when the body turned up. At the same time, though, I wanted her to be found so it would be over and done. So the drowning could be made official. I kept picturing her, that last flash of her white back, huge and fishlike, sinking under the beautiful dark green.

I had dreams about her. Like one time I was swimming in the surf and saw her rolling over in a wave, bloated, with Payne's dick between her teeth. It had a ragged end and I thought, no, Christ, no, they'll never be able to reattach it.

We didn't change our habits much during the day, but after the first two weeks I started going to Payne's at night. If anybody saw me, we figured it would just seem natural that he needed some company now that he was all alone.

Except for the bad dreams and waiting for Brenda to float ashore, I was pretty much living it up. The house was a mansion and I could help myself to a few of Brenda's little toiletries and her lacy stuff, things people wouldn't see.

Some nights Payne would bring home a big steak for himself and fresh swordfish or tuna for me. It didn't even taste like fish, or even like the fish sticks I used to eat. More like steak. He'd put it on the gas grill, and we'd drink some dry white wine and watch the food cook. He didn't drink much but he knew all about wines. I'd make us a salad and we'd eat at a little table by the pool. He had citronella candles to keep the mosquitoes away if it was a real still night.

I never knew the good life before, in my past always staying in apartments or sleeping on a couch in a place with a bunch of people. I didn't have much experience with luxury and privacy and regular food. I felt content except for thinking of Brenda once in a while, wondering if she had contributed anything to my food while it was still swimming. I would've probably given up the fish if it wasn't so sweet of Payne to buy it for me.

He said we had to wait a little while before we fucked—out of respect. I knew he was kind of religious being brought up Catholic, so it made sense. I was dying for it, but I told him, "Sure, baby, what do you think I am."

That next Saturday night was the beginning of a holiday weekend for us—Memorial Day was Monday. We didn't have to see anybody for the two days and I was oozing in my panties for some of him. I figured he was waiting till then. It would be the beginning of the good times.

I was right. He started on me in the shower after work. He slipped the soap between my legs and swirled it around my ass and up my spine. I put my head back and let the water take everything away with that soap.

He used one of Brenda's big pink towels and dried my tits and wrapped me up. He hoisted me against his chest and carried me into bed, nuzzling my neck all the way.

"I'm ready for the heavy artillery," I told him. "Gimme your big gun."

He got an amused look on his face and reached under the bed. He groped for a second and pulled out a rectangular black box. He opened the lid, and there in the middle of a dark red velvet cushion was a Dan Wesson .44 magnum with a four-inch barrel and six-inch and eight-inch extra barrels in their slots next to it.

"Holy fuckin shit," I said. I laughed.

I recognized what it was because my dad had guns when I was a kid. Not a magnum but lots of other ones. The smell of the gun oil brought it all back. Shooting was about the only thing we did together, besides look through the gun catalogs. When I got older I kept my interest in the guns on

TV. I was real high when I watched *Dirty Harry*, but I still recognized Harry's choice when I saw it gleaming up at me from its box.

I watched while Payne lifted it up careful, with two hands underneath pointing it away, and picked the bullets out of the cylinder until all six were plunked onto the beige sheet, shining next to an embroidered rose M.

"Unreal," I said. "It's fanfuckintastic, baby." I stroked the thick, stainless steel, satin-finish barrel very light with the backs of my fingers so as not to leave moisture from my fingertips. It was kept nice, pure class with polished walnut grips.

"I never thought of you hiding a big piece under your bed too," I said. "You're full of surprises."

"I've had it for a few years," he said. "My uncle was a collector. He always did things in a big way. When he died I got to choose something for myself and I took the gun. 'The Mahoneys are the best,' he always said, 'so they should have the biggest and the best.' The kit's valued at more than a thousand. It was just one of his toys. I never showed it to anybody before."

"Jesus, what do you do with a thing this size?"

"I've never done anything with it, but I can think of something," he said.

I was squatting on my knees next to him, and he tilted the gun up and placed the cool tip of the barrel against my pussy, pointing it towards my backbone. It took the breath right out and I felt a little scared of the hard metal. Then he started to move it real gentle. He rubbed it side to side and it did feel mighty good. I leaned back and propped myself against my arms. He started to work it in and out. I could feel the sight against my clit. The metal felt hard and soft at the same time. I arched my back and lifted and dropped myself, gripping the cold steel. I didn't worry anymore about moisture. Payne wasn't worried. He looked like he'd found a new thrill. I let it flow.

"You're one sick kitten," he said.

"No, baby. Umm. It just feels good." I was slow catching my breath. I looked at him. I saw something raw and sexy that I didn't know about. He was a spoiled rich boy and he could do what he wanted now. I could live with that. He put the gun in its box and set it on the nightstand. It was beautiful. I would remember to clean it. He put his own hard piece inside me. I came again. I lost count.

Two more weeks went by and we were still waiting for news about Brenda. Even a month later she hadn't floated up or blown in, or whatever it was she should have done. We'd fooled around with the throat douche for nothing. Payne said the scavengers were taking care of her. It was good and bad.

We kept up the sad talk about her probable drowning. Payne was getting touchy about the whole thing, but gradually the subject got to be less and less on everybody's mind, including the cops. Payne quit calling them, and they pretty much stopped coming around.

Rent came due on my efficiency for the second time since Brenda was gone and I convinced him I should let the place go and move in with him. Nobody had any suspicions I knew of. The other employees were happy to have Payne for their boss. They'd probably always hoped Brenda's drinking would do her in.

I fit all my clothes into one suitcase and left the couple glasses and pieces of silverware I had, along with the mattress and end table. Payne didn't need the stuff at his place. He had everything, including gadgets I never heard of. I figured maybe the landlord could leave my things for the next person and save them a trip to the thrift shop. I took my little driftwood lamp because it was special. Payne said we could put it on the screen porch.

Everything went just fine, except for my bad dreams and hardly getting laid. Payne was worried and worn **out** because he had to work extra to keep up without Brenda. He was gone a lot too, being busy with details on the new store. Some nights he'd get home late and be dog-tired and he wouldn't touch me. Sometimes it stretched into three days. He wouldn't touch me around work at all. I missed doing it between the drapes in the back of the shop the most.

"You get it in the king-size bed," he said. "There's no reason to risk it on the concrete floor."

He just couldn't see it. The work was taking some of the growl out of the animal. But he still had that sweet, innocent face.

I got into the habit of going out behind the house on the beach in the morning before work, early. Payne said he'd always done it. For me it was brand-new to get out of bed before eleven to do something I didn't have to do. We'd take a long walk up and down the beach in the surf. Payne would grab a swim, but I didn't want to get into the water with my nightmares.

I'd take a second walk and catch a little sun while he swam. I liked to strut my stuff and watch the old men drool while their wives bent over to pick at the broken pieces of seashells. They looked like sandpipers with their bony legs holding up round jutting stomachs. They were rich enough, they should've bought their pretty shells in the shops like Payne did.

I remembered when I lived in Cleveland I heard about the piles of spiral shells and giant conchs waiting to be scooped up off white sand beaches. But then it's never true. I got out West once and expected to find cattle skulls blazing white under those giant-armed cactus in the desert. But I didn't recognize the desert, even when I passed out on it. The Everglades ditto when I saw the long stretches of weeds. It looked like fields. I knew there was water under there, but you could've fooled me.

Payne told me Sanibel had thousands of seashells and pure white sand. He said we'd drive there one day and I'd see. It was worth a try. It sounded like heaven to go there with Payne. And Brenda wouldn't be able to follow me over to the white sand.

I walked below the weed line and trashy stuff left by high tide past the private beaches. I thought about Brenda as the foam swirled around my ankles. It always happened when I was by myself. I pictured her bloated body chugging along with the streaming black hair, like some wormy giant grouper, waves just breaking over her on the surface, little nibblers picking away at her in the shadow underneath. She was gradually mixing in, adding her juices to the pollution. A cool breeze fanned up goose bumps on my arms.

A hairy old pot-bellied guy swiveled on his legs like a radar dish. He was tracking my nipples outlined on the white bikini top. Poor old fuck. I put my hand under my hair and pulled out the neck bow in the back and then the midriff string and let the top fall into my other hand. Why not? The guy's mouth dropped open. I stretched my back and shoulders and raised my arms toward him and the sun. I used my free hand to fondle the right tit, and then did the left one nice and slow. A man and woman in front of me looked up from their shell picking and stared.

I took one more stretch and then tied the top on backwards and turned it around and put each of those babies back into their thin triangles. I liked the weight of them, the firmness. I added a little extra bounce to my step when I passed by and watched the oldies look at my sturdy ass in the G-string bottom. There was some kind of pleasure in it for all of us.

I got to the public beach and I spread my pink-and-rose-striped towel on the sand where it was firm and still damp and laid down on my stomach and took my top off so I wouldn't get a line. I wished I could pull the G-string off too.

I spotted a nice couple without kids. He was stretched out on the blanket and she was kneeling next to him, laughing. They were close to me, but I couldn't hear what they were saying with the waves rolling in. They were dark tan and their hair was the same color of brown, and full and curly. They looked the same age and the same size, even moved the same. But they didn't act like twins. She rubbed oil on his back and he rubbed oil on her stomach and grabbed her left tit inside her suit and rolled over and stuck his face down on it. They were the only people on the beach for all they knew. They were together. Just had each other and there wasn't anything else. Just like me and Payne.

They stood up and I saw they were deformed. Their arms were too long for their bodies, their hands too big, and their rib cages stuck out like they just took a big hit off a joint and were holding in the smoke. They walked stiff and wobbly, like toys, down to the surf, but their puffed out chests seemed proud. They didn't act different from anybody else. I guess they'd stopped worrying about anything. I told myself right then that I would do the same.

One night Payne brought home Chinese food. We were living it up. I used to say if I had twenty dollars to spend in a day, I'd spend a dollar on food and nineteen on drink. If I had a hundred I'd get some good drugs and forget to eat. Now I was starting to have food preferences. I never had won ton or moo goo before, but I took right to it. I ate the tiny corn cobs with chopsticks and picked out the crunchy vegetables around the bits of meat. I dropped a big sweet 'n sour shrimp on the carpet and Payne teased me about being a klutz. I'd pictured that shrimp nibbling on Brenda. She was sneaking up on me, but I pushed her away.

"It's no shrimp," I said. "How can you call something the size of a chicken leg a shrimp?"

His cheeks were puffed out with food and his soft lips shiny with oil. I reached over and pulled down his zipper and wiggled him out.

"Now, there's a shrimp," I said. But it was heading toward the size of a turkey leg before I could finish the words. Speed was one of his best qualities.

I waited till he chewed and swallowed. "Enough seafood," I said. I wasn't wearing anything so he just pulled me over on top of him and I banged down hard and long while I mashed his slippery sweet 'n sour lips.

For dessert I tasted a chip off the edge of a fortune cookie, but I didn't like it. Too sickening sweet. Payne broke his open.

"You are beautifull with two '*l*'s,'" he read. He tossed a piece of the cookie into his mouth. "I got yours," he said, "but they don't know how to spell."

"Well, if it's for me, spelling doesn't matter." I crushed mine to powder and picked out the fortune. "This one's yours—'You will have success in whatever you choose.'" I showed him the white paper strip. "These aren't real fortunes. They're already true." I poked around in the paper bag on the table.

"We are still fortunate," I said. I picked up the last one and tore off the crackly cellophane. "They gave us one extra. This must be our real fortune. 'The best profit of the future is the past.' I don't get it. What's it mean?"

He looked at it. "I'm not sure," he said. "They can't even spell."

thirteen

TWO MONTHS LATER BRENDA WAS STILL MISSING.

I was working the desk up front. Payne was off on errands at the other building. He was always off on errands there or somewhere else. Working the desk was boring even though I was temporary manager. I could fill in for anybody on break if there was a rush order, and I knew all the stains and what kind of removers to use if somebody asked me.

Marisol and the rest liked me because I wasn't a boss peeking over their shoulders when they punched in or checking up behind them to see if they'd tightened up loose buttons. I think it was too late in life for me to learn that attitude. I didn't give a fuck enough for a piece of cloth to get panicky about it. Clothing care was a funny job for me since I'd rather wear bare skin than raw silk any day. I did want Payne's business to do good, but I knew it would keep on without a lot of horseshit out of me.

I'd gotten a little half pint of schnapps that I tucked under the counter on its back behind the rolls of tickets. Just for a really small sip once in a while. It wasn't a habit— but I had to hide it because Payne didn't like me drinking during work. I sucked on peppermint lifesavers sometimes, so he couldn't tell the difference when he kissed me.

I was just screwing the lid back on the schnapps when Brian opened the door. I nearly lost my grip. He was a blond hunk of a surfer, a few years older than Payne. I knew him from Bubbles. He was my friend Nicole's old man and one time we'd fucked him together. It was his idea, but we all had a good time. Nicole and me sucked each other's tits and licked pussy like he said, and we both came before he even got his turn.

He walked up grinning and I looked at those tan muscular arms with the silky golden hairs. I remembered his red pubic hair and Nicole's satin black skin shining above him. A vacation smell of coconut oil floated in.

"Hey, Cherry, it's good to see you," he said. He flipped back a piece of blond hair that fell in front of his left eye. It fell right back.

"It's Sherri now," I said. "I gave up the Cherry a while back."

"Yeah, I guess. I'm still Brian Ball, you know." He winked and laughed low in his throat. "I wondered where you'd gotten to by now. I've been keeping an eye out in the clubs, but I didn't think to look at the dry cleaners."

He slung a bundle of clothes on the counter and I started to write it up. It was women's clothes.

"How's Nicole?" I asked.

"That was going to be my question."

"Oh."

"We split up about six months ago. I thought you two were good friends."

"We were. We just lost touch," I said.

"What about your old man?"

"Gone."

"Yeah. About time. You never knew how to pick men."

"I know," I said. I figured I didn't need to go into it all. "And you're gonna tell me that us two would've made a good pair."

"Yeah, why not?" he said. "I would have treated you more like you deserved."

"Come on, you were tight with Nicole."

He put out his hand and touched my chin and smoothed some hair back from my face while I stared at him. He looked into my eyes. It was probably the first time he'd seen me in normal clothes. I figured he never noticed I had a face before. "Well, I'm glad my mom asked me to drop off her stuff. I've thought about you quite a bit."

"Jesus," I said. Another one, I thought. I took a breath. "What?"

"Nothin. I just never thought of you having a mother around." I looked at the clothes. I'd learned to recognize designer stuff. "One with money."

He shrugged his right shoulder. "Everybody has a mother. It's fathers that are in short supply. How about meeting me somewhere tonight for a drink?"

"I can't. I've got something going. But it's good to see you." I smoothed some of his forearm hair with my finger. "Real good." I didn't want to start talking about Payne. "You're still keepin up your tan." I handed him his tickets. "It'll be ready on Wednesday."

"I'll see you then," he said. "Maybe we can get together."

I should have told him to forget it, but instead I watched those broad shoulders and armpits with the fine golden hairs flared out in the sunlight. He let the door close soft behind him. I caught his profile and the glint of the tiny gold cross in his ear when he took a left to head for the parking lot.

Wednesday morning I woke up wondering about seeing him. I put together a thin cotton shirt and the shortest shorts of my work clothes. I wasn't after Brian or anything like that. I just wanted him to see how good I still looked, parade around a little and watch the eyes follow the nipples. It could liven up a dull day.

It was really hot by noon, and when nobody was looking I'd stick my hand in the scoop neck to mop out between my tits even though the shirt was so thin. I felt half-drowned. Sweat was rolling down underneath. My skin was slippery against itself because I didn't have on a bra and I could feel the heat from my neck in Brenda's braided gold chain. Payne had said I could borrow it. I played with it, twisted it around my index finger until the finger turned purple to the first joint. It was something to do besides melt.

I was looking at the traffic, propped on the counter on my elbows when Brian turned up. He had on some low-slung baggies that would have looked like shit on anybody else, but the soft ridge of blond hair creeping over the waistband under his navel took my breath out. I didn't even mind the fat green fish running nose to ass around his legs.

I felt my hips twitch and the muscles start to tighten between my thighs. It was always like that with me. I would feel my body react and then I'd figure out the cause.

"How's it going," he said.

"A little hot today."

"Yeah? No air in here."

"You said it. It gets smothering sometimes."

He handed me his tickets and I punched the first number into the computer—six, nine. I laughed. I hadn't noticed when I gave it to him. The rack started to whir and move and the shifting snaky mass of plastic-covered clothes swooped across above us and fanned down a breeze. I felt goose bumps come up on my arms, but it wasn't cool.

I twisted and reached for his three items in a row, three expensive-looking women's suits. I guessed Brian for a typical South Florida boy. Money, toys, no real job, surfing, tennis, and golf when he wasn't in a bar or a strip club. But I didn't really know about his life except for the surfing and his mother's clothes. Maybe I wasn't being fair.

"So's your lunch break coming up?" he asked me.

"I just came in about half an hour ago."

"Oh, I was going to try to get you out for a beer over on the beach. There's a nice breeze from the west. The ocean's glass. No good for surfing, but beautiful for a drink—or lunch. I thought it would be fun to talk about the old days."

"We never had any old days. A couple of old nights maybe—when Nicole slid off and I took my turn."

"Come on, Cherry. It was more than that. We spent a lot of nights drinking together after work. And we went out for breakfast."

"Sherri," I said.

"Those were some great times. You two were crazy. Remember the time you got into an argument in the restaurant and both took off your shirts?"

"No. I don't doubt it, but I don't remember," I said. I

heard the glass door open up and I looked over to see an old woman coming in a slow hobble toward the desk.

"You were arguing over whose nipples were larger. They were so close to the same size you had to press them against each other to tell. Remember? The old guy in the booth across the aisle—his eyeballs nearly dropped out into his eggs."

"Who won?"

"You did."

"I wish I remembered. Sounds like fun."

"Well, I remember plenty. And when I think back to those days I always wonder why Nicole was the one I got serious with when you and I really got along better."

The lady was standing a few feet behind him, and I knew she was going to start having a fit if I didn't get to her fast.

"Okay, if you want, I can have a beer with you later. I can take an hour off around three," I said. "Is that enough time to swing by the beach?"

"Sure. Anyway I know a nice place on the Intracoastal that's closer."

I wondered what happened to the idea of seeing the peaceful ocean, but I let it go. I needed some air.

He picked up the suits and swung em around holding the hangers casual-like behind his shoulder. Everything about him had a sort of graceful swoosh. I felt a twinge between my legs just thinking about it. I wondered if I could catch Payne before I took off, work a little bit of the energy out of me.

"See you at three," he said. He looked liquid when he slipped through the glass door.

At three Marisol took over the counter and I stepped out the front door. Payne was still gone on his errands so I hadn't had the chance to try for a quickie in his office or mention I was going out. Brian stopped at the curb in his shiny black pickup and I took a giant step up into the cab. It felt good to be swept away from that shop for a while.

He stuck out his hand to help me in, but I landed on the seat with no problem. "It's jacked up for the big tires," he said. "I do some off-the-road driving once in a while."

"I can handle it, Brian. It hasn't been that long since I stepped up on a stage, you know." I rubbed my fingers over the creamy sheepskin seat cover. "You have a nice soft seat," I said.

We stopped at the place on the Intracoastal instead of going all the way to the beach. It was nice on the narrow wood dock over the water. We sat at a picnic table under an umbrella and ordered a pitcher. I only took one glance down at the water to see if there was anything bloated.

He was really getting into the old times. I missed Nicole, too, so it was good to talk about her. We had a couple glasses of beer and then he scooted around to my side of the table. Before I could do much thinking about it Brian had his fingers under the table worked up the leg of my shorts and inside my pussy. I felt myself melting right down. I started thinking of reasons for him to stop but none of em came out of my mouth. Payne's been neglecting me, I thought. All work. It felt damn good, but I wasn't gonna go any farther.

"Ready to ride?" he said.

I knew what he meant, both ways. But I gave him a half-closed-eye nod and said, "Yeah. It's time for me to get back to work."

All my feeling was below the waist. I took a breath and pulled myself up off the chair. He dropped some money on the table and we were gone.

The walk got my circulation going again. I laughed at his

bumper sticker when we got close to the pickup. "If it swells ride it." I'd seen it around town before, but never took it as a personal invitation.

"I sure don't want to go. But it's time for me to get back to work."

He didn't say anything, just opened the door on my side. I stepped up and he gave me a little boost on the ass and one finger went right onto my pussy that was so sensitive under the shorts. It just took my breath right out.

I had my hand still holding the armrest to close the door, but he took my fingers off it and climbed right in on top of me. I couldn't help feeling his hard dick pressing against my thigh through his jeans. I just had to give up trying to keep him off. I was thinking I wouldn't let him put it in. I just didn't know how to stop right at that second. I wished I'd never left the shop. I wasn't in control of my body.

He unbottoned my shirt and got his mouth on my tits and my nipples were stuck out a mile. We pulled down our pants and he slid it right in. It was damn hard and wide and I thought that a few strokes couldn't hurt anybody. Nobody would have believed it from looking at me, but I really didn't want to do it. It was just too late to stop.

We were parked in a shady spot and his windows were tinted black and just cracked at the top so nobody could see in if it mattered. He kept working and working it. His hands were under my hair and his face rested against my head. I was dripping sweat. Electric waves rolled over me. I moaned. I started feeling guilty about Payne as soon as I could think.

Afterwards Brian opened the windows halfway and reached into his cooler on the floor to get us each a beer. They were ice cold long-neck Buds and I tried to think of how good the beer tasted instead of feeling bad about

Payne. We just sat there naked for a minute and sucked on em.

"Same old Brian Ball, huh?" he said. "Just like old times, huh?"

"Not really," I said. "No Nicole." The beer wasn't helping and I was coming down off the whole thing and thinking, shit, now I'm going to have to lie to Payne. I really didn't want to do it.

"That's all right," he said. "We can make some old times for the future."

"Sounds good to me," I said, but I knew I couldn't ride that wave again. I felt awful. I figured it out right then that I was never gonna fit with Payne if I didn't change my ways. I was just going to have to control myself, not take chances. No matter what. He was worth it. It all went with cleaning up my life.

When I got back from my break almost an hour late, Payne's car was in the lot. I decided to forget the punch clock so he wouldn't see the exact time when he looked at the cards. I forgot pretty often anyway. I went right to the ladies' room and peed and wiped off from Brian and rinsed my face and neck, then went to find Payne. I looked through the little window into his office and saw him tapping away at the computer. I turned the knob quiet and snuck in behind him, stuck my face into the back of his soft neck, and gave him a nibble. He didn't flinch. His skin tasted salty and smelled good, like the animal he was when he wasn't worrying himself to death.

"I heard you sneak in," he said.

He didn't look up and he wasn't mad sounding, so I figured he hadn't been back long. He must not have noticed my punch-out. I was relieved.

"I think it's time for us to go on a vacation," I said. It

struck me that I wanted to leave town. Get another start on the clean life. I'd be gone if Brian stopped in. Somebody could tell him I was off with Payne. "I wanna see the real Florida—the way you're always tellin me—instead of this tropical New York City."

"We can't," he said. "Not now. You know better than to even ask me."

"I don't know. Why not? We could go to Key West. You're always saying how you'd love to go to Key West."

"Not now."

"Wouldn't this be a good time? It's off season. Business is slow. What's that fancy hotel you stayed in?" It flashed in my mind that he must have been there with Brenda, but I pushed it away.

"Pier House." He went back to pecking at the keys like the discussion was ended. He was working back and forth from his ledger to the keys and not looking up. Nothing mattered in the whole world except getting those numbers typed in. Maybe he just didn't care how long I was gone. Well, I'd think of it as a break. The last one I'd need. I deserved to be punished for what I did so I was getting off real easy. I would work harder to be the best at my job, so he would have a reason to love me and need me. And I would never fuck anybody else, ever. Next time I saw Brian I'd tell him to get lost. Tell him how in love I was with Payne. It was all decided. Not another single lie, nothing to hurt my sweet Payne.

I gave him a hug and kissed him quick on the cheek.

He looked up. "You smell like beer," he said.

I shut my mouth to stop the breath. "Sorry. It's just so damn hot today. I had a couple to cool off."

"I thought you'd stopped doing that. Is that all the respect you give your job?"

"No. It was only a couple."

"So, what if the customers smelled it?"

I wanted to say, so what—remember your mother? But I didn't dare. He was already getting worked up.

I felt jittery and hot. I didn't need any stupid questions. I'd already decided to change my ways and do everything for him. I looked at his red face and stepped to the side. I figured I'd get out of there so he'd cool down. He wouldn't follow me through the shop.

When I took the next step he grabbed me by the back of the hair, twisting it, yanking it up high to the side, pulling my neck back till I could feel the strain go from the back of my neck to the top of my skull. It hurt. Then he pulled me to him. I was shaky but I went for his mouth with my lips and I thought I was going to get it. I opened up ready. His hand came up and slapped me. It wasn't hard, but I felt tears trying to come.

"So where were you all this time?" He held me by the hair and said it right into my face. I caught some of his breath.

"I'm sorry. Down the street at Red's. I didn't notice the time. It was so nice and cool."

I knew if I told him I'd been at Red's he'd zero in on the place and not think about anything else. He hated that bar because of his mother going there. I didn't want to lie, but I had to. It was the last one. I'd already made the mistake, but I'd never do it again.

"I won't stand for that," he said. He pulled harder. "You hear me—I won't stand for it." He let go and his hand went down to my neck.

It didn't make sense but all of a sudden I felt like I was in one of the fights he'd had with Brenda. His voice sounded the same. I felt disgusted with myself. And sad. I just wanted to kiss him and hold him and tell the truth, but I couldn't.

He stared at me with his blue, cold eyes and I looked up sheepish. Then he pulled me into him and I knew it was okay. He was hard from my hip squirming against him.

I heard the hiss of the pressing machine closest to his office where somebody had started to work, but he pushed my shoulder down until he had me on the cool concrete. Then I wanted more than his mouth. He unzipped my shorts and peeled them off with one hand, and dropped his own pants to his knees. The keys and change jangled in his pockets. Nobody could work me like Payne. I was never gonna test my luck again.

Afterwards he went back to the computer. I went up front and took a teeny swig of the schnapps. I could still feel the sting between my legs. Payne could grind me to the bone.

No more fucking around. No more lies. I would never do anything that made me lie. I felt purified with Payne's come washing out Brian's.

fourteen

THE NEXT DAY THE PHONE RANG WHILE WE WERE
still in bed. It was one of those calls with timing,
coming when he'd just rolled off me and I was still dazed,
stuffed with cotton. I lunged across the bed and picked up
the phone. It got the blood flowing into other parts of my
body, being that the cops were asking to talk to Payne.
While he listened his face bleached white. When he hung
up he told me a body had washed up in Broward County—
female. He had to take a ride to the medical examiner's to
see if it was Brenda. He would go to the store and open up
and get things rolling, then take off for Broward. I could
go in at my usual time and take over from there.

He got dressed fast.

"I have some rush paperwork to do first," he said.

I kept noticing, alive or dead, how she could put a hop into his step. I rolled over into his spot and pulled the sheet up to smell what was left of his clean scent and fall back asleep. I should have known better because the ocean closed over me in a dream that stuck with me for the rest of the day like sour beer or the stench that clung to Payne later that afternoon.

The dream started in the waves where I saw the police pull her out. She was covered with weed and had tiny green phosphorescent fish stuck in her black hair, like in a net. Payne had told me about those sparkly fish from a documentary, so I guess that's why they turned up in my dream. They were like jewelry on her, and she was beautiful, not how I expected. Payne came up and took her and carried her away and left me there.

I was drowning. Every time I stood up another wave knocked me down and the undertow dragged me farther out. I could feel slimy tentacles tangling around my ankles. Payne never looked back. He kept carrying her away, into one of those rose-colored sunsets you see when you're caught in traffic on I-95.

Then I was with them in the hospital. I didn't see myself. I just saw him standing over her. She was flat on the table naked. Her eyes were wide open and dark green. Her big tits were pointing up at him and her legs were spread out with the tiny emerald fish sparkling and wriggling in her pubic hair, tangled in the tight curls, beautiful, like on her head.

I kept trying to scream to Payne, "Don't touch her. Don't touch her," but he was bending closer and closer. I could only make a croaking noise in my throat too low for him to hear. He looked at her lovingly and put his mouth on hers in a long kiss. I knew his tongue was in her and then hers was in him. I saw him bite hard and a dark stream of blood run down her neck and puddle between her tits and her stomach. He took to licking the blood and suckling those breasts and rubbing his face on her. All the while I couldn't move.

They got up after a while and walked past me hand in hand. Payne was smiling. Brenda turned back to stare at me and she had that ragged-end dick in her mouth again, sticking it out at me like a tongue.

I jerked awake and ran into the shower. But I couldn't soap that picture out of my mind.

Later that morning I was working the front counter when I heard Payne's footsteps. I smelled the rank odor on him before he got to me, but he looked like he needed a kiss so I took his head in my hands and kissed his mouth and pressed my cheek hard against his.

"It wasn't her," he said. "It was another dark-haired woman. The cops said the woman had only been in the water for three days, so I knew it couldn't be her, but I had to go through with it for show."

"What did she look like?" I asked. "Did she drown?"

He couldn't answer right away. His nice lips were bunched up like he couldn't unstick em.

"Shot. In the head. Looked bad," he said. "Horrible."

I thought of my father. How I imagined he looked. I never went to see him blind and mute and fed through a tube. Just heard about him from a family friend. He had such a hard time—where Hank and Brenda went so easy.

"Was it a drug deal, you think?"

"I guess. The cops thought so. I don't know." He started swallowing like his mouth was real dry. "She was big, full of gases. Her face was so puffed up you couldn't see her eyes. Skin was peeling off in patches. I could see the splintered bone in the bullet hole and—I don't want to think about it." He swallowed again. "The smell was the worst. I can't tell you how horrible it was."

"I know," I said. "It's still all over you. I don't know how you keep from gagging. Why don't you take off your clothes and dump em in the dry cleaning machine? You can clean up in the men's room and put on some stuff that isn't due for pickup today."

He was afraid to do it. He said he thought the smell might stay in the fluid and contaminate all the other clothes that ran through, even though the chemicals were constantly filtered.

"No, we had some cat urine in there one time and people complained for days. I don't want to risk this."

I thought maybe he was too prissy to wear somebody else's clothes, but what did I know? He could afford not to. He decided to go home and take a shower, and that seemed a good idea at the time, but he left me standing there by myself still smelling the odor of death that clung to my face where I'd laid it against his.

He didn't come back to the store that day, and I didn't blame him. I just caught the snags and closed up that night.

When I got home at nine-thirty he wasn't there. The house was dark. I dragged off my sweaty work clothes and Radar came into the bedroom and barked at me a couple times. I went to the kitchen and looked in his food bowl. It was empty and the water bowl was almost dry. I filled them up and took a beer out back to sit on the patio and let the salt breeze tickle my tender parts.

The waves were barely lapping at the wide summertime beach. I liked the winter beach better with the sharp slope and big rollers; it was wild—alive. The wind would whip your ass pink and keep you moving. But the calm beach was soothing to live next to. Except thinking that Brenda was out there.

Radar came over and sniffed my crotch. I started to wonder what Payne did with the foul pants and shirt. Then I thought about what he said. The body at the morgue got coughed up in just a few days but already the skin was peeling off. That meant the last crumbs of Brenda must've been scavenged weeks ago. There couldn't be anything left for that old ocean to spit back. There was no way. No reason to keep checking the surface for her dark jagged silhouette.

I went back into the kitchen, tossed the empty, and opened the refrigerator. There was at least a six-pack spread around the shelves, Heineken and some other foreign beers Payne bought because they cost more. He counted them every morning to make sure I wasn't overdoing it. None of em tasted much different. I grabbed another one, jerked off the cap, and went out to the patio and sat back down. I had it all. Everything I needed. Except where was Payne?

I listened to the slow quiet rhythm and sucked on the beer and told myself this was nice. This was the kind of life I always wanted. I was settled.

After a while, I didn't feel like sitting in the chair any more. I took my beer into the bedroom, set it on the night table, and plopped down on the cool sheets. The ceiling fan was moving the chilly air across my nipples and I rubbed my thumbs over em and tickled myself, circling my fingertips around and around the white meat I got from wearing my top too much. The tits almost glowed white against the tan. So where was Payne? I looked at the clock. It was ten-thirty.

I reached under the left side of the bed and pulled out the black box with his .44 magnum. It had felt so good the day we met. I tilted the lid up slow, smelling the gun oil and feeling like I was getting into something I shouldn't, even though he never said so. I hoisted it out of its velvet and turned it to the side checking for ammo. Sure enough, he always kept it loaded. I picked out the six bullets and dropped them on the bed. I was sitting on the edge and I looked down at my pretty two-tone crotch and decided to give er a go. Why not? Payne had started me on it.

I picked up one of the bullets and felt the pleasure of it in my hand, the concentrated weight in my palm. I put it in the chamber and felt myself smile and chew my lip while I clicked the cylinder around, once, twice, round and round. I nested its nose under the pubic hair and stroked. I wondered why I was doing it, daring fate. It didn't take me long. I held my breath and came with a long, low groan. I knew I couldn't lose. It was the way things were going. I meant to finish with a click of the trigger—but I didn't. I wasn't sure of nothing, even in my floating brain.

fifteen

 HAD THE BULLETS PUT AWAY AND WAS BUFFING UP the magnum when I heard Payne open the door. He walked into the bedroom with a shine on his eyes, a real hard gloss. I thought about all his errands and how tired they made him. He looked pretty sleepy, but I couldn't think of any errands he might have been doing that late. I buffed hard at the gun. I couldn't form the words to accuse him. I didn't want to hear myself say them.

He looked at the floor. His voice was shaking. "You're going to have to leave," he said. His arms were across his chest and his shoulder gave a little twitch and he moved his eyes to my face. "You have to move out of here. I can't live like this anymore."

"Like what?" I asked him. "Christ's sake." For a second I

thought he meant I shouldn't be using all his stuff and playing with his gun.

"It's like I condone it. I've been thinking about this for weeks. I did wrong to help you. I was scared. I can't live like this anymore."

That almost knocked me down. It didn't make any sense after how well things had been going. "No!" I screamed. "Don't even say that. I did it for you. I changed my whole life. I made a new life for us. It's been good."

He just stood there looking at me.

I felt like I was losing it. "I love you. I love you, baby." I focused on the full, firm lips that had said those words against me and I felt some kind of a red hot bubble blow up inside my chest. I started to try to figure what the whole thing was about. It came to me right away with a jab inside my stomach.

"Where were you, Payne? You tell me who you've been fuckin." Christ. Jesus Christ was all I could think. Some other woman got a hold of him.

"You're crazy," he said. "You're fucking crazy. You think that's all there is? Don't you have a conscience? You probably never even heard that word before. You think I'm out fucking around? I'm suffering. Can't you see I'm suffering because you killed my mother? I'm living with my mother's murderer."

I wanted to say something about how he hated her. That they never had a nice word for each other. That she made him fuck her, for Christ's sake. But I couldn't get any words out. I just sat there with my mouth clamped.

"You don't even care. I can't live like this seeing you enjoying yourself on my mother's money."

"Money?" I screamed. "It's not fair! I did it for you. So she'd stop hurtin you. For us to be together. You know how

it happened, almost by itself, like we both agreed. Listen to
me, baby—"

"No. No, I can't. You have to leave. I have to think."

That made me good and mad—him having to think, me
having to leave. It was too late for that. He should've
turned me in the night it happened.

I still had the gun close by and I grabbed it and put my
finger on the trigger. I raised the heavy piece way up and
aimed, sighted right at his lips and made him close em
tight. He was about fifteen feet away from me and I could
see the shine go off those eyes and his light tan bleach
lighter.

"Listen," I said. "Listen to this, son of a bitch—" I cut it
off. No use. What was I gonna say? I couldn't stay with him
if he didn't want me.

I held the line steady on those lips and pictured them
splattered to pulp. It hurt like hell to think about it, but I
wanted to squeeze that trigger. He stood stiff. I watched
him holding his breath. I squeezed. It clicked. I dropped
the gun on the bed.

"I'll go," I said. "I don't need your sorry ass." I wondered
what I'd've done if the bullets hadn't already been stowed
in the box.

He sat down real fast on the floor and let out some air.
"You bitch," he said. He sat there looking at me.

"I'll be out of your way by tonight." I managed to keep
my voice from cracking. "I can always find a place to go.
Who you got movin in here?"

"Nobody," he said. All of the wind was let out of him.
"You have it wrong. Nobody. I just can't be with you now,
with everything you've done."

"You helped me. It worked out right. We were happy."

"I've never been happy. I've been suffering constantly.
You just never noticed."

"Why didn't you tell me? I can make it better, Payne."

"No, you can't." He looked down at his fancy boots. "I won't lie. There was a girl tonight—who I talked to. She used to work for me. But I'm not interested in her body. Sex isn't everything in life, regardless of what you think. I ran into her a few days ago. She saw the change in me right away. She could tell something was wrong. She said I needed time to get over my mother's death. She's right. And I can't do that with you. I have to be away from it all."

He went on and on about his guilt and how he loved me, but it was killing him. He'd bought some bullshit and gotten stuck in it.

"I need to go to confession to be forgiven, heal myself, but I can't—ever—because I can't tell the priest what you did."

Then I understood the problem. He was too full of religious guilt and rules to let it all go. He didn't understand how his mother had controlled him or that he would've never been free. Just lying to the police was hard on him. The sweetness I loved—I murdered to save—was going to take him away from me.

He ended up telling me there was some sort of monster between us. That I could agree with, but not the way he meant it like a sin.

"Who is this girl?" I remembered what I'd heard from Marisol at work when I first started there. "She the one Brenda burned?"

"No. Somebody else. I ran into her. That's all. She's not the problem. She just made me think."

"She's the problem. We were fine."

"I've never been fine. I thought maybe I could hide it. The shock would wear off, and I would feel better. But it isn't working. You keep reminding me of it all. I have to do something before I kill myself." He pulled himself up, leaning on the side of a chair. "You have to go," he said. "But you can stay the night. I'll get a hotel."

He walked out. I listened to his feet click across the tile, the front door open and close, and the car start up and pull away.

I felt mechanical. I went into the kitchen and reached into the bottom cabinet behind the spare sack of dog food and got out a pint of Jack Daniels I'd been saving. I needed to sip some and think of what I was going to do.

I never went to bed the whole night. I might've dozed, but I was still sitting up when it got light. My mouth tasted bitter. Even dawn light hurt my eyes. Fuck his conscience. I packed the few clothes I'd brought and stowed some of Brenda's lacy panties in the bottom of the suitcase I was borrowing. I'd gotten rid of all my panties—they had holes. I just sat in the stuffed chair in the bedroom and waited.

It was still early morning when Payne came back and I hadn't thought of anything to do.

"There's no hurry," he said. "I don't want to throw you out. I want you to stay and work for me and look for a nice place. I'm just confused."

"That's not what it sounded like last night," I said. "I'm so grateful I could spit."

He took a breath. "Can't we talk about it? Be nice?"

"You can talk," I said. "This is your house, as I'm sure reminded, and you can stand here and work your jaw all day if you want and make yourself feel better, but I was told to beat my ass out the door. I don't need to be told again. You can start lookin for my replacement at the shop too."

He started talking all kinds of stuff about being sorry and confused, just needing time, but it wasn't worth listening to. When you had what we had and when your feelings could grab you around the throat the way ours did, I didn't see how anything else mattered.

I closed the suitcase with the little that was in it and walked out. I passed Radar in the hall looking at me. I felt my eyes fill up and had to just keep going. I made sure my heels clicked across the tile like Payne's had, and I didn't slam the door.

sixteen

I DROVE INTO THE NEIGHBORHOOD WHERE I KNEW Brian lived. I'd checked the phone book for his address. I couldn't remember it from being there only once or twice. I didn't have any trouble remembering his name, just one Brian Ball in North Miami.

I found the street and the number. The house was real small compared to Payne's and the yard was a jungle instead of a perfect trimmed lawn. It seemed a little familiar. It looked comfortable. Safe.

His truck was in the carport but it was only seven-thirty so I decided to wait a while and then knock on his door. Unless he had a guest in there it wouldn't be a problem. He'd be glad to see me. If he did have a thing going, I'd blow it off and swing on over to Bubbles to see who had a free couch for a couple nights. But I was determined not to go back to dancing.

It was pretty stupid, but I hadn't kept my paychecks since I moved in with Payne. It'd made me feel like I was putting my share into the household. It wasn't a big share, but now it seemed like a lot since I'd left with just a twenty in my purse.

I looked down at the clothes I had on and thought about what I'd packed, what few things I actually owned, mostly work clothes, some secondhand underwear, and a couple G-strings left from dancing. For all my hard work I had the same as when I'd first stepped into that dry cleaners.

I had the radio on but wasn't really listening until I heard the D. J. say it was the morning after a full moon. I wasn't superstitious, but I wondered if that had anything to do with Payne's deciding to throw me out. Never can tell. That moon might have put out just the extra vibrations to make him take that step.

The only thing that mattered was losing Payne. I'd thought I had enough shit in my life that no man could do me in—wrong. So wrong. So so wrong.

I sat there and let myself dwell on those lips. Remembering the feel of em made me think I might just as well take a sharp turn into a canal. Brenda could have her revenge. I could grab a current towards the ocean and stew in Brenda's soup, in peace under the smooth surface.

I might have thought more about it, figured out a plan to end it some way—I don't know—but fate took over cause Brian opened the door and jerked his head, seeing me sitting there on the street. He was wearing a skimpy pair of white nylon shorts. The sun in his gold hair gleamed up the contrast of his smooth tan and those clingy shorts. He caught my attention even the way I was feeling.

He bent down to pick up the newspaper and dropped it behind him into the house, then strolled down the path barefoot and graceful.

"Hi, sweet thing. You're up early this morning." His hair fell across his forehead and he ran it back with his fingers and then stroked down his unshaved chin.

"Do you have half a bed I can borrow for a little while? If not, just say so and I've got another spot. No reason to beat around the bush."

"I've never been much of a beater-around-the-bush myself," he said. "Rather get right into the bush." He tilted his head through the open car window and kissed me on the forehead. "Got a suitcase?"

He carried the bag and held the door open for me and I tried to act normal and keep that hangdog look off my face that I could feel sitting behind my eyebrows.

I didn't remember the inside of his place from before. I'd been pretty high and not interested in the surroundings. There wasn't any air conditioning, but he had ceiling fans. The living room furniture was a batch of end tables, a greenish leather couch, a huge-screen TV with a video player, and against the far wall heading into the kitchen, stereo equipment with monster-size speakers. Rod Stewart was already gutting out something low.

There was no carpet, just the smooth, stained terrazzo floor, old Florida style. He had some beer posters on the wall, with Coors, Heineken, and a lot of colorful surfboards. There was one I'd seen in bars of three girls side by side on a towel. They had on bathing suit patterns that matched up like a puzzle to form the Budweiser label. I didn't see any feminine touches around, no fancy pillows or curtains. The room was dark and cool from the shade of jungle plants and palms outside the open windows. It would suit me fine for a few days—until I could figure things out.

"I'll put your suitcase in the bedroom here," he said.

There was a clump of clothes on the terrazzo in front of the door. He stepped over it and I followed him past another TV and a king-size waterbed. He put the suitcase down by the bed.

The bed was rumpled but the striped sheets looked soft and tempting since I hadn't got any sleep. I sat down on the padded edge.

"Mind if I take a little nap? I don't feel like I can be good company right now." I looked up at him. "Better for you to jump me later."

"Sure. Whatever you want. Go right ahead," he said. "Sleep all day if you want. Actually you're not looking the best I've ever seen you." He put his arm around my shoulder and squeezed.

"Fuck you very much," I said and scrunched my face up at him like a little kid.

"I was thinking of taking a ride down to the beach to check out the waves. I'll tell you what. I'll bring us some lunch later, and we can eat it here in the sack and watch *People's Court* or something, if you're not too dragged out."

"That'd be real nice," I said.

"Sure thing, sweetheart." He moved that tan body out into the hall.

While I was taking my shoes off I listened to him getting stuff together in the other room. He opened the door and closed and locked it behind him. Brian was really a nice guy.

I flopped back on the cool swell of the sheets and caught his scent in the pillow. It was sweet and mildly sweaty. The ceiling fan turned slow enough to see each blade. The breeze was soft. The slosh of the bed felt comfortable when I curled over on my side.

I woke up and looked at the digital clock on the night-stand, already two-thirty-five. It hit me strange until I realized it wasn't Payne's clock. I was at Brian's. It was an awful jolt. I felt more beat down than before, feverish and sweaty. I felt like I was drugged—almost. I would have liked to been.

I could feel tears behind my eyes as I pulled myself up and walked down the hall. I found the bathroom and stepped into the shower. I'd made it a point that nobody ever saw me cry since I was a kid, since old Darrell. He saw me cry over a horse, not a man.

I let the tears flow with the shower and tightened my body into rock. I put my forehead against the tile and pressed, pressed hard. I had so much pressure on the inside I thought I might burst my lungs. I wished I would. Then all the pain would stop. Payne. I kept on and on, hoping I might die, but I didn't, and after a while I knew I couldn't.

I'd found a damp towel on the back of the toilet and was drying with it when I heard Brian come in.

He yelled my name from the hall. "I got us some lunch."

I wrapped the towel around my hair and headed into the living room.

He was pulling white paper packages out of a sack, setting them on one of the end tables. He stared up at my bare tits for a second before he opened the side of one package. It was fish with crunchy brown coating and lettuce and tomato. He pointed to it. "You like grouper?"

Grouper still reminded me of Brenda and her bloated shape under water, and I hadn't wanted it since that night, but I took a good look at it and decided right then to eat er up and flush er down.

"You're a doll," I said. I put my face into his and gave him a kiss.

He stayed on my mouth sucking in my lips one by one, and lowered the hand without the fish to dip a finger between my legs. He rolled my clit around and I could feel the juices start to flow, even though my mind felt numb. He took the finger out and sucked it.

"Tastierrr," he said, putting a growl on the end of it. "How about an hors d'oeuvre?" He licked my ear. "A quickie appetizer?"

I smiled and put my face in his for another kiss. I wasn't really hungry. I figured I might as well make him feel good. I wished I could lose my mind.

He dropped the sandwich back in the bag and was on his knees burying his face in my bush before I could move. I let him get a good long slurp before I pulled him up and towards the bedroom to ride the waves.

Afterwards we ate our grouper sandwiches and all I tasted was light crunchy fish and tartar sauce, nothing bitter to choke me. It felt comfortable with Brian. I decided I could stay for a while and let things settle. Then maybe Payne would miss me. I could go back to my old job and my lover. Start living again.

In a few days I knew Brian for a real sweetie, pure natural—he just wasn't Payne. Brian took life easy. He'd get up early and spend the whole day on the beach, or else wear his bathing suit under his pants and say he was going out to show some property—real estate. He'd come back later with his shirt and pants on his arm and sand on his ankles. I didn't know for sure where he got his money—maybe he could make a sale when he needed it. He always had enough for food and beer for both of us. He was happy to take care of my needs, but I started thinking of putting in some applications, if I could figure out what kind of work to try next.

Brian had a great sense of humor and being with him was how I'd spent most of my life, living day to day or high to high—except the food was better. We'd go to the beach, eat, drink, fuck. But there wasn't anything between us besides fun—a lot of it. He was a real joker in bed. He was big and could stay hard forever, so he fooled around a lot, teasing and hiding it from me when he could see I was dying for him to plug it in.

One time he tucked his dick underneath his thighs and closed em tight so he had just a skimpy triangle of pubic hair showing.

"Oops," he said. "Now you'll just have to do me like one of your little girlfriends."

"Okay," I said, and I rubbed my nose in the small clump of fur and nipped his thighs and licked in all the cracks. His hard-on popped right out in my face.

I put on a little girl's voice. I'd played the part before. "My, my, what a big pecker you have, granny!"

"All the better to fuck you with, my dear." He growled and grabbed me and pushed my hips forward until I lowered down on his stiff cock, riding with my back to him till I finished him off.

I raised up and watched his wet cock plop out onto his thigh. I bent forward and looked between my legs at his face. "You don't scare me," I said. "The big bad wolf is dead."

He opened his eyes. "I bet nobody scares you—except maybe Payne. Old Payne-in-the-ass? That's what we called him in high school."

"That pisses me off," I said. He'd mentioned before about knowing Payne in high school. "Why'd you bring him up?" I was sorry I'd told him anything about us. "You don't know what you're talkin about," I said.

"I know plenty. And I know how you're mooning over him. I've seen your eyes. You're dying to go back with him, the shit. He's got some kind of a thing—a bungie cord— on you, around your neck. I don't understand it. I knew him well enough in high school. Never liked him."

"High school's a long way back."

"Somebody gets you busted, you remember it." He shook his head. "He wasn't in my class, but he had a locker next to mine. Looking back—he probably caused me to drop out."

"You've gotta be mistaken," I said. "Payne wouldn't do that, not on purpose anyway."

"Trust me, sweetheart. He'd screw his own mother out of her last quarter—maybe he did."

"Shut up," I said. "Don't say another word." I was shocked at Brian's strong feelings. And I didn't want to talk about Brenda. "You got him wrong. You must have smoked out your memory a long time ago."

"I still see him around town once in a while. Thinks he's hot shit."

He looked at me and rubbed at his eyebrow.

"When I read about his mother in the paper I wondered. I figured she had a lot of money—"

"Son of a bitch. She didn't have anything besides the business. He was already an equal partner. There wasn't any other money. Even the stupid cops realized that. He has to work extra hard now to keep the place goin and afford his house."

"Why doesn't he sell some of his property?"

"There's no property. It's just a small yard. You can't sell off the beach."

"No. I know that. I thought I remembered his mother buying some property a while back. She was working with somebody from my office. Could be the deal never went through."

"It must've been the new store," I said. "So far that's nothing but a headache."

"Yeah, probably. Anyway, she was a lush. I wasn't really surprised when she drowned."

I took a breath. "That's what everybody said. Payne still had a rough time of it though. He loved his mother."

"Well, I'm afraid I won't be wasting any tears on him. He's a user in my book."

I didn't say anything. I figured he was either confused or he wanted to make me distrust Payne so he could keep me for himself. Slim chance he'd seen Payne around town since Payne hardly went anywhere. I looked at Brian with my mouth clamped. I just wanted to drop the subject.

I said, "Yeah, you're right. I can sure pick em."

I laid myself back on the pillow and rolled over to face the other wall. He let it go. He was a nice guy. He had a great fucking body. None of that mattered. I didn't love him.

I planned to make my break the following Sunday. It was the best day of the week to talk to Payne. If he wasn't ready to take me back, I'd ask him for enough money to get an efficiency for a couple weeks and food. He owed me that much in paychecks. But I really wanted to get him back. Help him feel better. I was sure he still loved me.

Saturday night I told Brian I was going to leave in the morning.

"I have to find out if things can be patched up with me and Payne. I just can't give up that easy," I said. "I should've listened to him more and tried to understand his problems."

I knew Brian disagreed, but he didn't put on any pressure.

"You're stuck on the bastard," he said. "If you have any trouble—or for any reason—just come on back."

I woke up around eight that morning and couldn't fall back to sleep. I put my head under the sheet and woke Brian real slow, until he was full up. He gave me a dandy farewell.

"'Preciate everything," I said.

He lifted his head off the pillow and shook it a little. "Watch out for the big bad wolf, sweetheart."

"I thought you were the wolf?"

"Just watch out. You know who I'm talking about."

He put his head back down on the pillow and closed his eyes and I picked up my clothes from the night before and tiptoed out to put em in my suitcase in the living room.

seventeen

B RIAN STAYED IN BED. I HEARD THE TV GO ON AFTER
a little while, but I didn't go back in. I had a shower and a donut, cleaned up a little, and left close to ten-
thirty. I hoped Payne would be alone, reading the paper on
the patio like he usually did on Sunday mornings.

On his street I drove past a dark-haired girl in a blue
Camaro headed the opposite way. It was silly, but I took a
look behind his car before I pulled up, to see if there were
any signs on the blacktop—like drip marks—of somebody
that just left. I couldn't tell. It wasn't my business since I
was gone, but I wondered if that girl he "talked to" might
have just crawled out of those rose-colored sheets.

I gave a quick knock and waited. He didn't come to the
door, so I used my key and walked in. I smelled the coffee

and then I saw him through the sliding doors, sitting on the patio. I glanced back toward the sink. Dirty cups and plates were stacked, so I still couldn't tell if she'd been there.

The whole place looked like a hurricane had ripped through. The cleaning woman must not've shown up on her day. Payne wouldn't think of straightening up or doing the dishes.

There was plenty of time in my life when I wouldn't have thought about that either. I wondered if being high on money was like being high on crack? Turned your feelings off to everything else. But Payne had feelings. I'd seen em. There was just always someone else to clean up for him. Why should he do it?

I slid the door back and stepped out. He was sipping a full cup of coffee, squinting at the front page of the paper, so he hadn't been reading long. Give it up, I told myself, before you find out something you don't wanna know.

I used my sweetest voice. "Hi," I said.

He jerked his head around and I saw the gloom parked on his eyebrows, but he started to smile when he looked at me, even seemed tickled.

"Hi," he said.

It came out low in a sort of heavy breath with a hush sound at the end of it. Like something sacred was happening, or precious. Then he remembered to get tough and glare at me.

"So where have you been? Don't you think you could have let me know?"

My face got hot. "Well, I didn't think you gave a fuck. You never asked where I was going."

"All I said was I needed some time. You ran off and hid."

"Are you crazy?" I said. He was trying to pretend I was the

one broke us up. I felt like I was dreaming the whole thing. Then it hit me that he couldn't admit being wrong. He'd never been alone before and he'd found out he loved me and didn't like living by himself. If he'd been with somebody, she didn't stack up. Our eyes locked and I saw he was really afraid to lose me. I felt like a little girl at Christmas, but I kept it covered.

"I wanna come back to work."

"I never expected you to quit in the first place."

"Are you nuts? You said 'out and gone.'"

"That's not right," he said. "You forced it. I was just asking for some time. I was confused. I never said anything about work. I wouldn't do that to you—besides . . . I need you."

"You know I need you too," I said. I took a hold of his hand and squeezed it. I took it up to my mouth and pressed the back of it hard against my lips. "I've been so miserable."

I could feel the warm softness fill up my chest—like I wanted to hug him forever. He needed me just how I needed him. Like I used to need coke. That bad. He wanted to pretend the awfulness between us never happened. That was fine with me.

"So does that mean you want me back at work?"

His eyebrows went up, like he just couldn't believe I was asking. "For heaven's sake, what do I have to say? Yes, get your beautiful ass back to work." He motioned toward the street. "Let's get your stuff and bring it home. I never really wanted you to leave and I don't want to talk any more about it."

"I brought my stuff along for the ride."

We walked through the house together and out to the car to get the suitcase, and he carried it back with one hand and put his other arm around me. God, he smelled sweet. I nuzzled my face into his neck. He kept his arm across my shoulder all the way into the house and stopped to kiss me twice. It was a total change. I wanted to know more of what happened, but I knew I shouldn't push it.

He shut the door and I petted the sweet Radar. "Nice boy," I said. "Did you miss me?" I scratched behind his ears.

"The police were over here," Payne said real quiet.

"To the house?"

"Yeah. I couldn't figure out what was going on. They were back asking questions—about my mother's assets—if she left any other property. I don't know why. We already went through all that. Did they talk to you?"

"No. 'Course not." I thought to myself it was funny that Brian had asked about property too, but I didn't want to bring him into the conversation. "How would they even know where I was? You didn't think I said something to the cops?"

"I didn't know what to think. You were pretty upset the last time I saw you."

"I'd never talk to a cop if I didn't have to. You ought to know that. And I'd protect you even if it meant turnin myself in." I looked at his innocent face. "Why worry? There's no other property. Is there?"

"No. Nothing. But you were acting crazy. I didn't know what you might have said. I thought I'd hear from you. I didn't know where to call."

"I'm sorry. Maybe I am crazy."

He picked the suitcase back up and headed for the bedroom. I was hanging onto his belt loop right behind him.

"Let me show you crazy," I said.

I grabbed him as soon as he got near the bed and latched right on to those lips. The pussy was already pumping heat, my knowing how bad he missed me. He pulled my head back with my hair and laid a bite on my neck. I yanked my shorts down and he lunged at me and dug like he was going for China. I didn't think that woman had been with him after all. I knew I was back where I should be.

The next morning I got up early and went out to sit on the patio. I was a little raw between the thighs and I laid back on the lounge and spread my legs to the breeze.

I looked out over the green chalky stretch of ocean and thought about Brenda floating lazy under the surface. It was warm pea soup and she was content in the cycle of things. I hoped maybe Payne had gotten over his guilt problem. It was good to have the sting back in my crotch. He seemed bigger and harder than ever.

Radar walked up and stuck his cold nose against my pussy and took a few licks. His tongue was soft. It was soothing. I'd missed his company too. I patted his head and he looked up at me with his innocent long-lashed eyes.

"Sweet baby," I said. I put my fingers into the silky fur behind his ears and rubbed.

He put his face back down and licked me a few more. There was some pleasure in it for both of us. He dropped down on the patio for a snooze, and I let my head loll back and felt the coolness of the air on my wet pussy and thighs.

Payne slid open the door. He'd just got out of bed and his hair was flopping all directions, but he looked as sexy as ever. He looked at the dog on the ground between my legs.

I smiled a big smile.

He sat down on the lounge next to me. "He was licking you, wasn't he?"

"Poor thing doesn't get much fun," I said.

"He used to do it to my mother when she'd pass out with her robe hanging open."

"Oh." It stopped me dead. I thought about Radar licking that black pussy and Payne watching. "Well, I guess I can't hold that against him. He didn't know any better."

"Anyway," Payne said, "I think we should get married."

"Huh?"

For a second it felt like the time I took one step too many backwards on a table top and landed on my ass.

"You serious?"

"Yes, I'm serious. I think we should make it legal and everything. Do it right and start clean, possibly even get married in my parish. I was thinking about it while you were gone."

I reached down and kneaded Radar's neck. He got up and walked over under a palm. An umph of air came out of him like it always did when he dropped his hulk on the ground.

"We're together. That's how it is, so we'll make it legal, under higher authority. Maybe in my parish church. We'll make a good life, take care of each other and forget everything."

As soon as he said "forget everything," all the details came back like bubbles in my stomach, one big misshapen bloat in my middle, a bloat with a pink plastic bag over her head who was a churchgoer.

"You want to get married? In a church? Christ. I never had much luck with marriage." It wasn't a cheerful idea to me. I'd tried it a couple times real young. If anything, that piece of paper seemed to chase the love away.

"Yeah. Catholic. Why not? Let's do this whole thing right. I used to go to church every Sunday with my mother. It's been six months. I miss it. We could start going together."

"I'm not Catholic."

"It doesn't matter. Anybody can go. You just can't receive communion."

"Well, I can't see me puttin on a hat to go to church every Sunday."

"You wouldn't have to. I just thought it would be nice to

be like a normal couple. And Jesus, nobody wears a hat that I know of."

It seemed like a weird idea to me. Something funny had got into him.

"I remember when I was little," I said, "we called the Catholic kids cat lickers. The girls always wore hats to church—or little fuckin veils. My friend had one with bows and polka dots that pulled down over her head like a bowl. The edge made little teeny patterns of squares on her upper lip. It looked silly to me. 'Course, she didn't think so."

I reached out and smoothed Payne's hair back. "I never had anything against cat lickers, but I don't need to be one."

"You wouldn't be one. We'll just have a nice church wedding. Then it'll be a legitimate marriage. Everything will look good. We'll be solid churchgoing citizens."

It seemed strange that he was becoming so outwardly religious all of a sudden. Maybe he was getting scared. I decided to drop it.

"I'll think about it," I said. I couldn't see myself going to church for appearances, like old Brenda.

I sat there dead quiet while he explained that if we got married he'd put me in a position in the company too and I would have a legal share. He'd work it all out. I'd never have to dance naked for a living again.

He was so cute about it all. I thought to myself that swaying my ass to the music was a whole lot easier than pumping steam, but my new life and my sweet Payne were worth it. I figured he was trying to make me secure and show his feelings.

"Everything that's mine will be yours," he said. "I don't want you to ever have to worry about money."

I thought, well, he didn't give that a mention before. But things were changed.

"So, what do you think?"

"You know, when I was married the last time it didn't take a month until he started tryin to tell me what to do and teach me lessons with a knuckle sandwich. That's where I lost this tooth. There was even worse stuff after that."

I'd never told him much about my past life, only hinted at what happened with Hank. I stopped talking and pointed to the empty space toward the back on the left side. "I lost this when he thought I called the cops on him."

I'd always wondered if Payne noticed the tooth. I figured if he was suggesting to marry me he ought to know just what he'd be getting and not getting.

"Oh well," he said. "Let's buy you a new one and then get married. The divorce was finalized and everything, right?"

"Oh, yeah," I said. "It was final." All I could think was how nasty things turned, no matter what you did. But that was in the old days, my other life. Payne was different. And Payne and me were already tied together for life anyhow. It didn't leave much room for choices.

"Don't get any ideas about me poppin out a kid," I said. "I can't."

"No way," he said. "I just want to start over. Making it legal will put everything right."

"You think so?"

"We can take a honeymoon. I'll take you down to Key West to the Pier House."

"I never had a honeymoon."

"Okay. That's what we'll do."

"If you really want to," I said. The honeymoon sounded nice, but I still hoped he would forget about the M-word.

eighteen

T WAS ONLY TWO WEEKS LATER I WOKE UP ON SAT-
urday morning and saw him clicking shut his suitcase.

"Bounce your skinny ass out of bed," he said. He bent
over the bed and gave my ass a slap on the right cheek.

"Ouch. You watch it or I'll grab your dick."

"Not this morning," he said. "I want you showered,
dressed, and packed in half an hour."

"No problem." I wasn't awake yet, but I thought, hell,
I'm game. "What's goin on?"

"We're headed down to Key West this morning—for our
honeymoon."

"We don't have to get married first?" I asked. It sounded
too good.

"We'll worry about that later. I went out early on the

beach and looked at the sky and thought, geez, it's just too nice to stay inside. Probably the last time I took a few days off was five years ago."

"What about the shop?"

"I'm going to run the keys over to Marisol. She can handle everything for a few days. We're closed tomorrow anyway. I figure we'll come back on Tuesday night and work like dogs the rest of the week. I'll tell her not to schedule any pickups until Wednesday afternoon."

"People might not want to wait that long."

"We could lose a few customers, but I don't think so. Most of them have been with us for years. We deserve to have a break."

"It seems awful funny," I said. "You didn't even close when Brenda died."

"Listen, you're the one who's been bugging me about going to Key West. Now get moving before I think twice about it."

"You sure are full of surprises."

He grabbed my hips and scooted me across the sheet to the edge of the bed and made me laugh. I could feel the wild blood pumping in my chest.

"I really don't have to go to work for three days?" I asked. I got silly and just stayed limp and made him pull me up by the arms. He got his hand in my hair and pulled my head back and gave me a kiss.

"Move your butt. In a few hours we can be in Key West sipping piña coladas." He motioned to the dresser. "Put on your bathing suit and some shorts in case we want to snorkel or get some sun on the way down."

"No problem." I was dressed in my bikini and shorts and packed in half an hour, and he was ready to go. I never saw him so excited about anything.

On the way we had to drop Radar at the kennel. He

looked so sad I felt rotten, but when we got on the turnpike with a cooler of beer and a bottle of champagne, I could feel the gloom just raising up off my eyebrows. I felt as light as the blue sky all around me. Even through my dark glasses the sun glittered so hard on the trees that the leaves flashed a silver lining.

It was the Florida I expected all along, and Payne was in the best mood I ever saw—I never would've thought he could forget work for a second. He put in a Jimmy Buffett tape and opened the windows and sang his heart out. It sounded so sweet. He said we were supposed to listen to Margaritaville music all the way to Key West, no news, and we weren't allowed to talk shop. It was okay with me.

I reached in the cooler and got us out two ice cold, dripping Coors. I felt the cleaning fumes clearing out of my brain and blowing away in the breeze.

Warning signs were posted along the road because it was only two lanes. They said, "Patience Pays," meaning to wait for the passing zone, but to me they were a personal message. I'd used my patience all right. Finally things were falling into place.

We came around a bend and the water spread out to the right and made me suck in air and fill up my chest. It was so blue, so sudden. The sign read "Lake Surprise," and I couldn't believe it. Everything was perfect.

I wanted to stop at one of the little bars along the way, but Payne didn't like the looks of em, not clean and shiny enough. We drove past all kinds of little homey places and mostly over sparkling water.

"I always thought you'd be able to tell somehow where the ocean stopped and the gulf started," I said. We were headed over the Seven Mile Bridge.

"Don't be silly. It's all the same, same water as on my beach."

"It looks bluer and clearer," I said.

I didn't want to think Brenda could've floated this far. Seemed like the whole world was going to be polluted by her. No, I told myself, some shark already ate er. She's long gone.

"Hey, see that nest between the telephone poles?"

"Yeah," I said. "It's humongous." I turned all the way around to get a good look as we passed. It was a big clump of sticks balanced on the cross-piece between the two poles. "What is it, baby?"

"Most people think they're eagle's nests, but really they're osprey." We passed another one. With a big bird in it. "See, there it is. It's an osprey, not an eagle."

We sped by and I couldn't see enough of it to tell. I wondered if ospreys had a beak like the spoonbill and Brenda. I still couldn't stop thinking about her. "You're so smart, Payne," I said. "I didn't know you studied birds."

"I haven't really studied them. I pick things up from magazines and TV." He tilted his chin back cocky. "But you'd be surprised what you don't know about me."

"I'm gonna stay around till I learn it all," I said. I reached down and unzipped him. He tightened his stomach for me to undo the button.

"Forever, baby," he said.

I reached in and pulled out his cock. It was already starting to swell when I scooted my ass toward the door and bent down to drag my lips over his satin smooth skin. I loved the feeling of it plumping up in my mouth. I figured the truck drivers got a kick. I sucked him dry.

It felt like a short ride. We drove straight to the Pier House and got ourselves a room. They said we were lucky to hit a cancellation. I never had a $230 room before. Payne just whipped out a credit card. It was the fanciest place I ever went. They even had tile on the outside floor.

The guy carried up our bags and Payne gave him five bucks. "The girls at Bubbles would love you," I said.

"Let's not talk about anything at home. I don't want to think about it. We're starting over now. This is going to be our honeymoon."

"Fine with me," I said. I looked in the bathroom and saw little bottles of free shampoo, and bar soap with jasmine scent from the Key West Fragrance Company. The toilet paper was folded into a neat point on the end. "Christ," I said, "Do I have to refold the ass-wipe every time I pee?"

Payne laughed. "You'd better." He was at the window, looking out. Our room was on the beach side. "Come over here," he said.

I was there in a flash, squinting at the bright water with my arm around his waist.

"Look. It's topless. You can show off your tits like you're always wanting to."

"Long as it's okay with you," I said.

"Everything's going to be okay."

We slept till ten the next morning. It was the latest Payne ever slept since I knew him and he woke up on his back, raising a pup tent. I climbed on and he worked me one way and the other, threw me around like a sack o' taters.

"You're a wild one this mornin," I said. I caught some breath. "A real devil." He flipped my ass over and pinned me to the bed again.

"You can take it, babe. We're a couple of little devils. We both enjoy the heat." He was different than I'd ever seen him. He even seemed smug—in charge. He lifted my hips and tore into me. I just wondered for a second what was in that Key West air.

It was almost noon when he went into the bathroom. I got at the room service menu and called in two orders of eggs and fresh fruit. It was my first time ever and I felt I handled it nice. I didn't have to order coffee because we had our own complimentary pot by the sink. I asked if they could bring a newspaper, and sure enough, they said they'd be glad to.

Payne came out of the shower and I took my turn. When I finished he was sitting at the table drinking coffee and chewing on some toast. I got myself a cup of coffee and sat down next to him.

"Where's the paper?" I asked. "Did you already read it and throw it away?"

"No, there's no newspaper."

"Well I asked for one and the guy said sure they'd bring it—just like I was the Queen of Sheba."

"They must have forgotten."

"I'll call and ask again," I said. "We can take it down to the beach and read it together."

"Never mind. It'll blow all over."

"I can handle it," I said. I picked up the receiver.

"No."

He grabbed the phone out of my hand and put it back down. "We don't need a newspaper. We're on vacation and I don't want to read about what's happening in the world. We're getting away from all that."

"For Christ's sake," I said. "It's no big deal."

"I don't know why you're so hot on reading the newspaper all of a sudden. Why do you want to sit around in the room waiting for a paper when we could be out on the beach?"

"Okay," I said. "Okay. Let's hit the beach."

We did. We hit the beach every day. For three days I oiled and tanned my tits. I watched the straight guys pretend not to look when I smoothed on the oil and made my nipples hard. The gays walked by not noticing.

We drank blender drinks that were like dessert. Payne

even drank plenty of em. I told him that was what made him so sweet. I could feel my body relax and fit into the habit of swimming and tanning and eating three meals a day. I never ate so good before. Or did souvenir shopping. Payne got a Jimmy Buffett T-shirt and I got a light pink one that said "Key West" in multi colors. It was cut into fringe from the ribs on down to let in a nice breeze. Payne said I just wanted it because if I stretched my arms up high enough my tits would stick out. I said, "So what."

I spent a lot of time just looking at Payne's beautiful face and touching the back of his soft neck. We fucked so many times my knees stayed weak. He did me on a beach chair down below our window and made me come sitting on a stool in the King Conch Saloon. My skirt was hiked up and he got his hand between my legs. I just sat there and melted, feeling a shit-eating grin on my face. The bartender didn't let on, but I know he figured out what we were doing.

It was only my second vacation ever. The other one with Hank I can't hardly count since we slept in the car most of the time and I got a shiner during it.

We were cheeseburgers in paradise, like Payne's shirt said. Until Payne checked his answering machine. He checked it every night, but this time there was a message from the cops. He got white and shaky even with his new tan.

"Don't worry about it," I told him. "They wouldn't've left a message if it was anything serious. It's just more routine."

That settled him down a little. "I guess you're right. I gave the hotel number to Marisol in case of emergency, so she would have called if they came to the shop."

"Sure. It's been a long time now. It's just some paperwork. It's been too long to be more questions about Brenda."

He just looked at me.

"Come on. I'm not worried," I said. "So why should you be?"

"Yeah," he said, but he was still white.

I opened us some wine we had on ice and in a few minutes I was feeling horny as usual. They couldn't spoil Key West.

I sprawled myself out ass up on the bed and called to Payne in the bathroom. "Come and do me a little doggie, baby. Pretty please. Just a quick dogger, Payne babe." I was hoping to bring him out of his mood.

After a few seconds he came strolling over, looking at me, but like he wasn't taking in the view.

"Do me with that jumbo mushroom," I said.

He looked down at his side and I saw he was holding the travel iron he'd brought along. I'd been making fun of him bringing it ever since I saw it in his suitcase. I couldn't believe he was going to primp up his clothes that late.

"If you're plannin to iron the sheets, babe, forget it, cause I'm not gettin up."

"Roll over and give me some room," he said. He was looking dead serious.

I rolled over on my side and he sat down next to me and plugged the iron into the wall socket by the bed. "I want you to do it for me," he said.

"What?" I asked him. "Iron the sheets?" I laughed, but I was real nervous.

"You killed her, so now you have to do it."

"What?" I said. But I knew. "No way," I said. I sat up and put my hands behind my hips.

He put the iron in front of me and jerked my arm from behind my back. I felt the strength he was willing to use on me. He took my hand and curled my fingers around the thin black handle. The iron was flimsy and collapsible, but I could feel the heat coming off it. I could smell the hot metal. He must have had it heating already in the bathroom.

"Put it away," I said. "I'm not gonna do anything like that."

"Yes, you will. You want me, you'll do it."

"Payne . . ."

"Do it," he said. "Just once. Against bad luck. Put it on the inside of my thigh."

I held in my breath.

"Now," he said. "Now."

He put some pressure on my hand and I pointed the iron down. I was just going to touch him with the tip fast so it would barely burn. I couldn't think what else to do.

Metal touched skin. I felt it stick. I tried to pull back but he pushed on my hand and I couldn't move. I looked up at his face and saw his clenched teeth and the tears running down. It was done. I'd done it. Just like she must have.

He lifted my hand and I saw the silver-pink triangle on his tan freckled thigh. He had me put the iron on the nightstand. My fingers were frozen around the handle. He pried them off one by one. Before I could say anything he was on my lap and my head was shoved back against the pillows. He was digging in. He jammed into me hard, but I couldn't feel it.

All I could do was watch that pearly sear move up and down, so close to touching my yellow-tanned hip. When he finished and fell asleep I cried.

He had his pants on in the morning before I opened my eyes. His face was stone cold. I stopped looking at it. We packed and drove straight back in silence.

When we got home Payne went to the police station. I

picked up Radar at the vet's. He was real glad to see me. I took him home and fed him and then drove to work to get started on the catch up. I said to myself, hell, what else could I do? I'd figure out a way to help Payne. I loved him to death.

In no time I had Marisol and the others busy on their jobs and was waiting on the first load of dry cleaning in the machine. Everything was back to normal. Steam hissed, handles clanked. The sound of rushing water cycled off and on. I was working out a wine stain on rayon, the remains of some other woman's good time, and worrying what Payne was doing so long at the police station. Finally he came walking up from the rear. He had his smug Key West face back again.

"It's okay. Just another body they were going to make me look at. I didn't have to though. Somebody else already identified it. I think it was yesterday and the cops just didn't bother to call me back."

"Figures," I said. "Assholes."

He went on to his office and I saw I'd got the stain out, and I started thinking about all the work piled up. It hardly seemed like I'd been gone except for that. At least it was Wednesday instead of Monday.

nineteen

PAYNE GAVE UP ON THE CHURCH IDEA FOR US GET-ting married. He said it would take too long and he didn't have the time to put into it. The new store was almost ready. In fact, he gave up the legal marriage idea altogether. It was fine with me. Odd how he changed his mind so quick, but if it meant the guilt routine was over and I didn't need to go to church, I was happy as a bug.

We picked the first Sunday after we got back to have our own little ceremony on the beach. We talked about inviting some people and having a party, but Payne only had distant relatives—he didn't want to invite employees—and the only close friends I had were a few people at Bubbles, and Brian.

I didn't dare mention him again. I'd told Payne about

him when we first got back together, but that was a big mistake because Payne kept bringing him up, saying how fast I slid my ass out of one bed into another. I thought to myself that it's not something you can use up, and besides, he drove me to it. But I didn't say nothing. Payne was so innocent about the world I couldn't blame him. I wished I could be more like he was. I didn't deserve to kiss those sweet lips. I just felt lucky Brian didn't turn up again at the shop.

So we did without the complications and the snoopers and made ourselves a pact under the full moon. We even got dressed up for the occasion. I had on a white, slinky, beaded dress that nobody'd picked up from the shop. Payne said I shouldn't wear all white, so I added a red leather belt of Brenda's and painted my toenails to match. He looked his coolest in tan cotton pants and a thin shirt half-buttoned. It billowed like a sail in the wind when we walked toward the surf.

The beach at night—without Brenda—was much prettier than being stuck in some stuffy church with a bunch of strangers glaring at your hairdo or something and listening to your promises that are none of their business.

"I promise to love, honor, cherish, and—" I laughed— "give you a blow job whenever you want. Till death do us part."

"Can't you be serious?"

"I am serious. Anytime you want."

"Okay." He picked up my hand and kissed it really sweet. "I promise to love, honor, and cherish you until death do us part."

He opened a box with satin inside, picked out the earrings he'd bought me, and put them real delicate through the holes in my ears. They were beautiful gold hoops that I said I'd wear instead of a ring because we decided not to mention around the shop that we were married. Payne said it was none of their business. I sure didn't care one way or the other.

I'd got him a new gold cross with money I saved from my checks since I started keeping em. He'd lost his old one. I fastened it around his beautiful smooth neck. He kissed my lips.

After the kiss I pulled my dress up over my head and helped him pull off his pants. I could barely see the burn scar in the moonlight. The stripping down was part of the ceremony. He said it was his first sex on the beach. He'd brought a cleaning bag to put our clothes in, so they wouldn't get messed. I got on my back to keep him off the wet sand. It was a thing with him, but I didn't mind a little grit. I came right when a wave lapped my toes. Then I came a few more times.

We rinsed off a little in the edge, but I didn't want to get in too far. I left my dress off since I was still wet and had sand stuck in every crack. Payne just put on his pants and we walked up to the house.

I looked at his smooth back shining in the moonlight in front of me and my footsteps felt light. I nearly floated up the rise toward home.

We started back into our old routine at the house, swimming and grilling out. I felt good being a wife to Payne. I was pretty much off the schnapps too. The only problem was his being tired out from working at the new store. Sometimes my body had to go three or four days without any hard attention—but I was handling it. When we did bang our bones together, they hit strong and solid, with lightning running through. Some of the highs were gone, but so were all the shit-ass lows.

One time I drove up to help Payne out at the new store.

We were putting some of the Miami clothes through there, to check out the equipment and get the employees started in the routine before the place really opened. He was so hyped up, I didn't stick around long. It made me nervous seeing him so edgy. He ran around shouting orders like he was the captain and the ship was ready to go down.

I even heard him yell at a girl for wearing her shorts too short. I couldn't see the problem. She had on sneakers and socks, just looked athletic, not like she was trying to peddle her ass or anything—just a freckle-face kid. Payne told me the Broward customers wouldn't like it if they saw her, so she might as well not pick up bad habits.

I hadn't trained this girl like I did the others, by starting them with me in Miami. She'd just gotten hired up there. I figured maybe she wasn't any good and that's why Payne was so pissy, but I felt sorry for her anyhow. I hoped he'd get over his nerves after the grand opening. I would feel better about visiting.

There wasn't much slack time till the opening. The new sprinklers had passed inspection with no problem. In less than a month the snags were worked out and the finishing touches put on. It was all pretty fancy. The customer service area was sectioned off and air conditioned to suit the ritzy area where it was located. There was a strip of grass and a row of ixoras across the front, and Payne had the whole place painted up that pussy-rose color.

"It's soothing for the nerves," he told me, "and it says 'Florida' to the tourists. They'll love it."

It said fucking "Brenda" to me. I was starting to have mixed feelings about that color.

I woke up to his loud voice that Saturday morning when the store was due to "grand open." I was on my side against him with one leg across his thighs.

"Roll over," he said. "I've got to move. My four cases of Beaujolais Nouveau are waiting to be picked up."

He flung my leg off and I felt my eyes pop open like he'd just poked me with a big one, but I figured he wasn't up for a bang with all he had to do. He'd decided to woo the new customers with the wine, and all kinds of cheese, and fruit and vegetables with dip—tropical stuff like papayas and hearts of palm. That's all I'd been hearing for two weeks. He'd even got some stinking caviar. We tried it the night before.

"It's okay," I said, "but I've had come that tastes a lot better. Specially yours. If I were you, I'd serve em come on a cracker."

He'd grabbed me by the hair and forced my head down to make a taste test. End of conversation for the night.

"We're all ready for the yuppies," he told me as soon as he saw my eyes were open. He was pulling underwear out of the drawer, getting ready for his shower. "All those laundered shirts and suits, the 'dress for success' clothes, 'power suits'—it's going to be fantastic."

He put the clothes down on the chair and opened a paper bag to show me rose napkins and matches with "Miami-Purity" inside a hanger printed in gold, the way it was on the sign. They were wrapped up in cellophane and tied with pink ribbons. It all seemed a little extreme to me.

"It's worth spending a little money for the expensive business we'll bring in," he said.

"Yeah, it's goin to be a regular dirt mine."

I asked why call it "Miami-Purity" when it's in Broward, but he told me that was the company name and he couldn't change it. I thought I smelled Brenda there again.

"My pussy's hot and juicy," I said, wiggling my ass on the sheets, hoping I might still get him for a quickie before his shower. I opened my legs so he could take a look.

"Isn't it always?" he said. He looked and smiled, but I could see it was just for politeness. He was thinking of the old Bozo-lay aging at the importer's.

I snapped my thighs shut. "You better get your ass movin out of here before your Bozo wine turns into vinegar."

He was glad to get off to work, and I thought, hell, whatever blows his pants down. I couldn't make it to the big ordeal myself since I had to handle the Miami cleaners for the busy Saturday hours. It didn't bother me a bit.

I got to the store plenty early for my first day as permanent manager. I went to the back door and put my key in the lock and looked up at the name "Miami-Purity," stenciled in black for deliveries. A few drips of paint had run down, and it didn't quite make the grade like the pretty imprints on the napkins and matches. 'Course, the fancy stuff was for the new place, but it was all Purity Inc. I wondered why we couldn't clean up the back a little. After all, that's where the purity part was supposed to be done. Being the new manager I thought I might be able to fix up a few things.

I thought of that saying—the first day of the rest of your life. This was the day. I opened the door. The air that hit me was warm and humid, but I felt a chill roll down my back. I was officially the manager. My first position with a name.

I turned on the lights and set the dry cleaning computer for the first load and turned the boiler on to get the steam cooking. I brought the change up front and counted it into the cash register, twenties, tens, fives, ones, quarters, dimes, nickels, pennies. I checked the register tape and cleaning tickets. Then I headed back to sit down with a bin of clothes to be sorted into repair and prespot. I was working at the spotting board before it was even time to open up.

Shit, I thought, all my life I'd been wondering how it was to be boss. There wasn't a hell of a lot to it. I could handle it, no problem. I squirted some Streepro on a blood spot, took the bone, and worked it in. It was a good-size stain on the lapel of a woman's suit jacket. I wondered if she'd gotten a bloody nose or maybe a bite on the lip. I couldn't picture a woman in a pink suit jacket getting either. Then again, before I worked at the cleaners I would've said those women didn't sweat.

At noon everything was running fine, pressers were hissing, steam was rolling, machines were banging, and I needed to get out of there for a little while. Take my lunch break. I thought I'd ride up to Broward and drop in on Payne. Then I thought again. Fuck. I couldn't spare the time. Why would I want to go up there and see all those socialites drooling wine on their silk shirts and suits and whatever? I gave him a call instead.

"It's going great," he said. "Really crowded. And we're getting the expensive work, just like I hoped."

I decided to drop into Red Sky's for lunch. It'd been a long time. After all, this was my first official day as manager. I deserved to celebrate.

Payne was still rattling on about business. "What do you think?" he asked.

"What, babe?"

"I said, you think Jan can handle it, if I go out to get more wine?"

"Yeah, sure. I trained her right. She can do everything I can. Almost."

He was too serious to catch the little joke.

"I guess I'll take off and get it then. This crowd is really sucking it up. They've almost polished off the fruit plate and caviar too."

"The caviar shouldn't be tough to replace. Just go in your office and whip some up like I told you."

"Real funny," he said.

I was happy the whole deal was turning out nice for him. I hung up and headed for a cold beer down the street.

twenty

RED SKY'S HADN'T CHANGED SINCE I'D BEEN THERE about six months before. A place like that doesn't, except for wreaths at Christmas and shamrocks for St. Pat's Day. No fancy napkins or matches, no pretending. I looked up at the brass plaque above the bar in front of me. I'd read it as many times as I'd been there: "Red sky at morning"—no warning for me. I'd never been a sailor, and besides, it was afternoon.

The cool dark was soothing. It was quiet. Just a few men and myself. I ordered a beer and sat there smoking, enjoying it, holding my head up with one elbow on the bar.

The door was to my left and I heard it open and glanced over. The sun streamed in behind a muscular blond in cut-offs. I felt myself take a quick breath. In that split second I thought it was Brian. He stopped to adjust his eyes and I saw the guy was a lot younger. Not a bad looker. He sat down a few seats from me at the bar.

I ordered another beer. The drafts were small and I could spend fifteen minutes more.

The bartender was washing some glasses in front of me and looked close. "Hey, haven't seen you for a while," he said.

"Yeah, I've been behavin myself. Today I'm celebratin a little bit."

"Sounds good."

The blond guy looked over. He swung his eyes from my tits down to my knees. "Whatcha celebrating?"

"New position. Manager."

"Well, let me buy you a drink." He motioned to the bartender. "Dan, set 'er up for another one."

Dan set a shot glass upside down by my beer. It looked real comforting and solid sitting there. I couldn't do much but finish the one I had and move on to the next. I figured I'd drink em quick and get back by one-thirty, just a little longer than my normal break time. It was a fringe benefit of being management.

The blond guy moved over to the stool next to me. I pulled out my cigarettes, offered him one, and lit one up for myself.

We both sat there smoking for a minute. I was putting the beer down in mouthfuls between puffs.

"You look familiar to me," he said.

"Yeah? I used to come here pretty often."

"No, I think maybe I've seen you dance."

"Either you did or you didn't," I said.

He stared between my legs.

I was a little pissed with his nerve, but the stronger feeling was the warmth creeping up from where he was staring.

"I'm sure I did," he said.

He edged a little closer, scooting the stool in jerks. I had on a short jean skirt and he got his right knee touching the inside of my bare thigh.

"Such a smart ass on three beers," he said.

"Always a smart ass," I threw it back. "Smart all over. That's why I'm manager down the street." I was feeling that knee on me. I held a cigarette casual-like in my fingers, but the heat was working its way up my gut into my backbone and turning to chills.

"Where's that?"

"Miami-Purity Dry Cleaners."

"You traded in your dancing costume to work behind a counter?"

"There wasn't much to trade," I said. I held my finger and thumb apart about an inch and a half, the width of my G-string. "I got a good deal. Anyhow, I could go back if I wanted to. That kind of job is always open." Shit, the guy didn't have a clue, but he sure had a nice crotch aiming at me below the bar. My eyes always seemed to draw towards the zipper area on a pair of jeans. Something real sexual about it.

"Yeah? What about staying in shape?" He put his hand on the inside of my thigh. "It'd be a shame to let these beauties go flabby."

He stroked back and forth making little shivers crawl inside my skirt up to my pussy.

"Not a chance," I said. "I get plenty exercise." It meant leave me alone, but I was getting that old feeling. It was making waves up from where I was sitting on the plastic covered stool, and I could feel my throat tightening up, my whole body getting stiff. I didn't want it, but that magnet heat—the kind that comes from just thinking about fucking somebody new—was pulling me over to his side of the stool. No way, I said to myself. You've got your new life. You're the boss. You're Payne's wife. I felt something grab my guts and squeeze. Christ. For all I knew Payne was pressing up some little yuppie lady's blouse with her still in it. My body was talking to me—trying to get my panties down for this one. But I was fighting it.

I picked up my draft and swallowed a gulp of cold beer. The glass was still a comfortable weight in my hand, near full. The third or fourth? I felt heavy fingers resting on my thigh. I really had to get going. I had to.

I picked up the hand and squeezed it and placed it against his crotch. He laughed and made some jerk off motions. I laughed and picked up the glass for another swallow of beer. I'd finish the last one and drink a schnapps to kill the beer smell. Then I'd go back and take over the counter for Marisol.

I was just into the schnapps when one of my favorite salsa tunes came on the jukebox. My body felt nice and light and I slid off the stool to catch the beat. It was still habit. I swayed my ass a little and it felt good.

I was the only woman in the crowd and pretty soon I was the center of attention. I danced myself up the steps onto the wood stage, pulsing to the jukebox, showing blondie how limber I was. He was clapping and swinging his shoulders.

"Go, go, go," came from the left side of the room. "Do it, do it." I slid my tight skirt up to the hips to hunch down forward and then snake up into a back bend till I touched my hands on the floor behind me. I had on some of Brenda's pink lace panties and they got a whistle. When I stood up I stuck my thumbs under the bottom of my skirt, holding it up to the waist, and strutted forward slow with my knees bent, following the beat with my hips.

Somebody yelled, "Show us your tits," and the echoes followed.

Naturally that's what I did. I turned my back to em and did a grind while I unbuttoned my blouse. I wasn't wearing a bra and I opened the buttons halfway to the waist and turned back around to let them get a good look at all the bounce that was still in me. I felt the cool sweep of air conditioning on my nipples that were already sensitive from rubbing against the shirt. I was feeling damn good and horny. It was a hell of a time.

After that some minutes got away from me, and the next time I thought about anything "Lucille" was playing on the jukebox and I was standing in a dark corner—with blondie's tongue in my mouth—tasting his whiskey. Or else the flavor was mine. His hand was putting a comfortable squeeze on my ass under the hiked skirt. Christ, I knew my lunch hour was long over. There was hardly anybody left in the bar.

I could feel my pussy cooling fast and his mouth just started tasting sour. I wanted to get the fuck out of there and back to the cleaners. What the hell was I doing? My first real day. If I was lucky I could slip back in and Payne would never know.

I unlocked my mouth and took a hold of the guy's wrist behind me. He looked at me surprised but loosened his grip on my ass, no problem, and I pulled my skirt down.

He pushed it back up. "What's the matter, baby? You're not going to run off on me? "

"Sorry, I have to, hon. Really. Sorry. I gotta get back to the job quick."

"Hell, I thought you were ready to spend the rest of the day and part of the night."

He was bent forward zipping his fly. I guessed my hand had been down there.

"I'm sorry, man. I lost track. I told you about my new position. I'll fuck it up if I don't get back there fast." I finished buttoning my blouse, smoothed the skirt, and gave him a kiss. "I might have already."

He stood there giving me a tough made-of-stone look, like he'd been mistreated but could handle it. He wasn't going to give me any trouble. I hated to run off and leave him feeling like that, but I couldn't do anything about it. The whole deal was a mistake.

"Maybe I'll see you here again some time." I hoped not, but you never know.

His head bobbed a little like he was letting it sink in. "Okay, pal," he said. He gave a short salute and clicked his heels together.

I started moving real fast at that. I couldn't blame him for his attitude, but I thought, Jesus, I must be crazy. I got Payne at home, pure and sweet as Ivory Snow, and here I am, risking everything, sucking on some hunk of driftwood with breath like rotten eggs.

I pulled into the back parking lot at the store and looked around for Payne's car even though there was no reason for him to be there. I was nervous as shit. Inside the door the time clock showed three-ten. I thanked God I didn't have to punch it anymore. I ran through the back toward my office trying to notice if everything seemed okay.

I banged my hip into the steam cabinet and it hurt, but I kept moving. I could hear the reclaimer going and the industrial-size washer. It all sounded normal. If I got away with it this time, I'd never let it happen again. If he asked me I would tell Payne about a little extra time I took for lunch, so I'd still be clean since my vow. As long as he didn't see me drunk and everything was all right, he'd forgive me. Just let everything be all right.

When I got to my office, I pulled a brush through my

hair, dropped my purse into the desk drawer, and headed out to the front. Marisol was punching buttons on the rack, and it started to make its circular roll. I watched the shiny pink bags flow by me and the sparkle of them gave me a good feeling like always—even along with the dizzies.

She rang up the bill and counted out the customer's change. Finally he left.

"Whew," she said, "remember that one day—you told me to tell . . . if you smell like liquor?"

"Great."

"I smelled you when you walked behind me. The liquor and smoke."

"Payne call?"

"No. Nobody asked for you. It was quiet all afternoon. I had no break though. It was to be at one-thirty."

"I'm sorry. Please don't mention it to anybody."

"I won't . . . but you look bad."

I looked down at my shirt and skirt. They seemed okay to me.

"The others will see your eyes. I think you are taking Brenda's place for sure."

That hit me hard. My hand sprang toward her face like I was going to slap her. But I didn't. I wasn't Brenda.

"Don't ever say that." I put my hand on her arm. "I don't want to hear her name. I just celebrated a little too much today. It's not going to happen again."

I pushed my hair back behind my ear. It felt sticky. I felt sweaty and dirty, off balance. I wasn't used to myself that way anymore since I'd got with Payne.

"Tell you what. I just need twenty minutes to get home and take a shower. If you can stand to wait, you can leave then, and I'll give you a two-hour break on Monday."

I knew Payne would be stopping by to pick up the

bank deposit after he closed the other store at six-thirty. I couldn't let him smell me like I was. He would forgive me the extra time if I seemed okay. I could shower and put some of Brenda's perfume on my neck and chest to hide the smell of alcohol when it started oozing out of my skin. I had some gum handy for my breath.

"How about it?"

"That will be good," she said and her eyes shined up. "I will have time to meet Javier if I leave early." She didn't see Javier much because of her strict father's rules, even her being nineteen.

I told her, "Sure, and take whatever time you need Monday. I'll fill in."

"Be careful driving," she said.

I was careful and it took just a few minutes until I pulled into the drive. I started unzipping my skirt when I got the door open. I petted Radar and had my blouse off before I made it to the bedroom. As soon as I was clean I could start all over.

I felt the humidity still hanging in the bedroom and smelled the shampoo from our morning showers. I'd never noticed that before, never been home in the afternoon. The bar soap was still slimy on the bottom when I grabbed it and I thought the air mustn't be turned up enough. I'd have to remember to fix it before I left, so Payne wouldn't figure I came home. No sense in drawing attention to all the time I'd spent off the job.

I lathered up, rubbed soap into my chest hard. I was going to get rid of that layer of bar stench if I had to scrape my tits raw. Fuck, it was so easy for Payne to stay straight and work hard, and be happy about it. I wondered if it was his Catholic school upbringing. Somehow Brenda's evil never managed to get inside of him. I thought a lot about what I did to her, but I couldn't feel sorry any more. It was the only important thing I ever did for anybody in my life. I knew it was right, even if the cops wouldn't think so. They didn't know anything. Payne wouldn't've had a chance without me. But, Jesus, I was such a fuck-up, I knew I didn't deserve him. Every chance that came along I let my body get ahead of me. It's like I didn't have any control over it at all.

twenty-one

I SOAPED AND RINSED MY HAIR THREE TIMES AND squeezed the water out with a towel. I figured it should have plenty of time to dry before Payne saw me. I put a bottle of Brenda's perfume in my purse. There was a lot of it to choose from still stored in the little antique cabinet in the bathroom. I didn't wear perfume, but if Payne noticed, I'd say it was for my special day, a first and a last. That was the solid truth.

I had to put the same clothes back on in case he remembered what I wore from the morning—I thought of my grandma. "Over fooey under hooey," she used to say. It meant if you put on clean clothes and perfume without taking a bath you were just covering up the foo-foo. She always made you wash in the end. I guessed I was doing it backwards, putting the fooey on top when I was clean, but I didn't have a choice. I sniffed down toward my shirt and only smelled a little smoke. I could've gotten that much in the ladies' room at work.

The drive back was fast, no problem. Marisol was sweet as could be when I walked up to the counter. "Much better," she said. "You smell very good."

I took over for her and tried to concentrate on straightening up instead of going nuts waiting to talk to Payne. It was rough. I knew he could have been ringing my office line, and if he asked me how long I was gone, I'd have to tell. I wasn't going to lie.

It was four-thirty and I told Marisol to leave. I took her place at the counter. That would help when Payne got there. The next two hours and a half crawled, but finally I heard the click of his boots heading towards the front. I was finishing up with a customer so I didn't turn to him right away. I sorted her clothes into the right bins until the woman was out the door.

"How's come you're on the desk so late?" He was in a good mood. He pursed those lips and I bent toward him and nipped the plump lower one. God, he was fucking sweet and cool after a day of hustling customers.

"Hi, baby. I let Marisol cut out early instead of taking lunch." I got out a quarter wrapper and started fumbling with sticking the quarters in. "How'd the afternoon go with the yuppies?"

"Great," he said. "We did enough volume today so if even half the customers come back we'll be in good shape."

He started going into how much was owed on equipment and the rent and utilities each month, and salaries, and unemployment insurance, all kinds of "invisible" costs, but he was bubbling all over, and I just counted my dimes and let him ramble. He was young enough to think life could still be one big bowl of rosebuds, and you only had to pick one and watch it bloom. I didn't remember ever being that young—my buds died on the vine—but it was nice seeing him so happy.

I'd wait to tell him about my little mistake later, when I was completely sober. I wasn't sneaking anymore. I wanted to take the blame I deserved, as long as we could still be together. I'd ask for my punishment. Beg for it. At least he didn't notice the perfume.

"How'd the new girl work out?" I asked.

"Fine," he said. "Just fine."

"Think she'll be able to handle the pressing?"

"Sure. Yeah." He looked into the cash register to see what I had left. "You about finished so we can get cleaned up and go eat? I think we should celebrate—some place nice on the water."

"Sounds good to me. What'd you say her name was?"

"Um. Kathy. Something like that." He touched his stomach. "I'm starved. You about ready to get out of here? Let me help you turn everything off in back."

We walked on back and I wondered how he could be so hungry after his all-day celebration. I guessed he didn't have much time to eat in all the rush. The thought of food made me woozy and I was getting a whopper headache, but I didn't wanna spoil his fun.

"Did you save us any of that Bozo-lay?" I asked. "We could have a little toast while we're gettin ready. I never got to taste it."

"The Beaujolais Nouveau? No, sorry. They drained every bottle."

"I guess it was good stuff."

"Yeah. But you don't like wine anyway. I'll split a beer with you while we get dressed."

He must've forgot I drank wine with him all the time, but

I wasn't gonna make it an issue. My mouth was so dry I could hardly swallow, so I thought, hell, I'm willing to split a beer. Hell, yes, I'd split anything for my Payne.

Later that night I told him a little of what I'd done that day, having a celebration drink and staying a tad longer than I planned, but everything went fine. I said I'd learned my lesson. No more fuck-ups. He took it all without a blink. Hardly seemed to pay attention. He said he was glad I told him, no harm done. I hugged him hard with relief and kept my breath behind him. He was so tickled with the new store that nothing could spoil his day. He didn't fuck me though. That was my punishment.

THE NEXT FEW MONTHS I EASED INTO MY JOB AS MANAGER without much trouble. Payne let me take care of everything without checking up behind me, and I liked that. It was mainly because he was so busy at the other store, but I felt good he trusted my ass. He worked late and came home tired and I was good and tired too. I was staying out of Red Sky's. It was my new life.

One morning I had to go in early by myself to get some stuff done. It was real peaceful. I stood up front at the computer buttons and pressed 300. That number was way in the back and I wanted to watch the rack make its long roll to bring it around. I got a thrill watching that rainbow glide in the dawn sun. Those rosy bags glowed. I watched the rack jerk, gather speed, and start to throw sparks of pink against the discolored walls. It was like the Fourth of July. All the dirt was settled in the metal drum, and my work shined in the pure plastic film. I had the young, sweet Payne to go home to when the day was done.

The sparkles lasted a few seconds, then a semi stalled in

the street and cut the light to gloom. He sat there and ground his engine and I went on back to do my work. I could catch the show any morning I wanted.

That afternoon I was working on some ink stains when I got a call from Jan—the girl I'd trained for Payne's store.

"How's it going?" she said. Her voice had a whisper to it.

"Goin fine. What's up?"

"Oh, shit," she said. "Shit. I—I can't—say it."

She started breathing hard into the phone. I could almost feel the heat coming off her. "Something happen to Payne? Is he hurt?"

"No. He's not hurt," she said. "He took off—with Katie."

"Whaddya mean?" I said. But I knew in a heartbeat. I hadn't let myself think about it, but something had been sitting on my stomach for weeks. "The new girl?"

"The redhead. Not really new. She used to work at your store in Miami—until she had an accident."

I could feel my stomach tighten. The thing inside swelled up like a huge bubble. Hot liquid rushed up to my throat. She was the girl Marisol had told me about a long time ago, even before I'd done Brenda. The girl Brenda burned with acid. "Where'd they go?"

"Your house, I think. I was behind the Dumpster smoking a cigarette. I heard her ask him. She said she'd always rather go to his house than a hotel."

Jan kept talking, telling me she'd had suspicions before, but she didn't know whether to say anything. He was a real son of a bitch, a real asshole, she said, but I couldn't agree with her. I couldn't put anything into words. My hand on the phone was shaking from gripping so hard. I had to move.

"You have a lot going for you," she said. "Take my word for it. He's a sleaze. Dump him."

"I have to go," I said. I hung up and got my purse out of the drawer.

I flew into the car and started it. There wasn't room for a clear thought in my head. I could see the two of them, her fresh young face under his glazed unfocused eyes, all his feeling concentrated in his cock. I could feel the heat myself. I was caught in some kind of hot swirling high.

When I pulled into the drive I saw I was too late. Or maybe too early. I couldn't figure it. They should have been there. If they were still on the way they'd see my car.

I pulled through the drive and onto the street. I drove around the corner, parked, and walked back. I had to move fast.

I opened the door and Radar was standing there to greet me. It was that second I realized he wasn't my dog anymore. I felt like a stranger walking in that front door. None of it was mine. There was no new life—never had been. I never had any control over it. Payne had lied and lied and lied.

I locked the door behind me and flew into the bedroom, went to the far side of the bed, and got down on my hands and knees. I reached under and felt the gun box, its cool smooth surface. I'd make that son of a bitch tell me all of it. I wanted to know exactly when he started up with her. Why. Why? That was the part I screamed out loud. Why? Radar sat down on the rug next to my feet and looked at me with those sad eyes. He'd known all along.

I had the gun in my hand. I'd cleaned and polished it and left it empty. I flipped out the cylinder and loaded it up. I'd show the bastard that the bullets were all in it this time and make him tell me everything. I wanted to see the suffering on his fucking pure white face.

I sat on the bed and waited. It couldn't be long. I felt jittery. My eyes bounced around the room making the Brenda colors swim. The pussy-rose cover on the bed, the rich beige initials, the pussy-rose walls. Payne had kept her colors everywhere. I never thought to ask him to change— to get rid of some of the reminders. I always told myself it wasn't important. Maybe inside I'd known there really wasn't a chance. He couldn't settle for me. I felt the thought burn through my stomach and I took the gun and went into the kitchen to get a drink, keeping an ear out for the car. No reason to hold back the drinking now. Payne, Christ. No more.

There wasn't any Jack or schnapps, nothing but wine. I'd gotten rid of everything else. That was when I thought I had somebody worth giving it all up for. I grabbed the wine bottle and slammed the cabinet door. My stomach was burning. I wanted to scream and cry and puke. But I wouldn't. I had to get back into that bedroom and wait for them. Surprise them, run her off for good, give him a scare he'd never forget. Make him tell me all about it. I couldn't think past that.

I sat down on the bed and took a drink off the bottle. I pictured them making their way slow to the bedroom, like in the movies. She'd be plastered to his lips and his hand would be opening her shirt, cupping her little breasts. He'd have a hard-on like I hadn't seen in months. I went over to the chair in the corner and sat down on the floor behind it with my legs tucked under me and the gun next to me. It was a big stuffed chair with a skirt and I could just fit. I'd stay hidden until they got far enough into the room—and naked. Then I'd point the gun at his face. I wanted to see him lose interest in her tits, watch his hard-on shrink back inside him to sit with the fear in his gut.

I waited sucking on that bottle and feeling my stomach

grind together, burning like I'd eaten glass. I wanted a smoke but didn't dare. I started thinking—hoping—the whole thing was a mistake. Then I heard his car pull up.

I put the bottle down and heard the clunks of doors and the sounds of their voices. Radar got up and went into the living room and I listened to his claws click across the tile as he headed to the front. I heard the key in the lock and not a sound out of Radar. He knew her well enough.

"Hi, sweet puppy," she said. Her voice seared into my gut. She was so young. A young girl. I wanted to know her. To find out what she had that I was lacking.

I heard them move toward the kitchen, his boot soles coming down hard and her light bounce. Tennis shoes, I remembered em from the shop, perfectly white with pink laces and thick matching socks. I heard somebody—probably Payne—digging in the silverware drawer and I figured her to be the one chinking glasses, getting them out of the cabinet. I heard the pop of a cork coming out of a bottle. Payne drinking during working hours—he said it made you too sleepy to do a good job. He wasn't so fucking concerned with the job anymore. I wondered how long he'd been faking it.

They weren't saying anything. I could hear them coming back slow. I pictured him holding the wine bottle and her hanging around his neck. I scooted the last half inch toward the wall so I was sure to be completely blocked. The acid in my stomach was still boiling but my ears were tuned to catch every word. I could feel hot wires of excitement holding me tight against the wall.

"Um, yummy," the girl said. They came into the room. Her voice was high-pitched and eager. I felt sorry for her. She was just trying to find something to live for. She picked him just like I did.

"Don't you remember—it's the Beaujolais Nouveau I had at the opening," he said, "I saved the one bottle for us."

"That's sweet," she said.

I dug my fingernails into my thighs. Sparks ran through my hairline to the back of my head. He'd lied to me even about that. It was worse than him screwing her. It was a plan, a lie to my face for a thing so small. He didn't give half a fuck for me if he would lie about that.

I heard the rustle of clothing, clink of a belt, a zip, those soft pleated pants I loved on him from the first time, dropping to the floor. I saw myself bury my face in his groin and then suck him in trying to get him all, to fill up the ache in my chest. I'd done it so many times.

The bed creaked. I knew he'd pulled her on top of him. I could hear some movements and imagined their mouths together and his finger working her clit. She would stay plastered on those lips. How could she help it? I didn't feel anything against her. She had to take her own ride.

I started thinking back, trying to figure out when it all started. He'd known her before he'd known me. I thought of all the times he'd been working so hard just like today. All the errands. Him telling me to leave.

But why take me in again? Pretend we had a marriage?

I thought about the day I came back from Brian's. I remembered when Payne was walking me to the car to get my suitcase. He told me the cops came to question him again while I was gone. Something to do with the cops. Maybe he never wanted me back at all. Maybe he was scared I'd run and leave him the blame. It would've worked easy. He'd needed me close to be safe. He should've known I'd take the electric chair to let him off.

A hot angry wave rolled over me—a purifying boil. I would have done anything for him before, not now.

They were fucking hard, breathing loud. The bed was creaking in rhythm. I knew the pace. I could feel the slamming in my own pussy, the fullness. He was holding himself back. Letting her have it like she wanted.

For months I'd been fucking to his rhythm. The whole time I thought I was making a good life for both of us I was just making him a life for himself. Making him a life. It played back to the music of the bed—him-a-life—him-a-life—him-a-life. Finally I heard his groan. The bed music stopped. I knew they'd have their eyes closed and I decided to peek. I had to see what they looked like all plastered together. See her.

I had my back against the wall so I used my thigh muscles to scoot up till my eyes were above the arm of the chair and I could get a view through the space between the arm and the flared back. My nose pressed against the soft cotton. I could see their heads and shoulders. He was half on top with his face above hers turned to the other wall and her red hair was spread out under his head on the pillow. It was something to look at, his shining dark hair and white skin against the bright orange of her. Then I caught the gleam of the cross he'd "lost." It was around her neck, resting against the pillow. The fuck.

She put her hand up to smooth his hair back behind his ear and that was when I spotted the acid scar, a pale blotch the size of an egg on the back of her hand. Okay. I'd known it. It was my best guess. But how long it had all gone on just kicked me in the gut.

I slid my back down the wall and took a breath. It was all I had left inside of me. I didn't have enough strength to stand up and make them face me.

"I love you," the girl said. "Say you love me."

"I love you."

It sounded flat until he dragged out the "you," like he was far away and then coming back just in time to put some feeling into it. I'd heard the tone. I used to think he was working out some important business detail in his head when he used it on me.

"I missed you so much after I quit the shop. Those months when you didn't come around—I didn't have a life. I just waited for you." She stopped, probably for a kiss. She was so innocent. Too innocent to be fucked up like me. "But now," she said, "we hardly see each other. When will we be together?"

"We're together," he said.

I wanted to scream out that he knew what she meant. We all knew. I recognized the words so well. And now I knew that it was never just me and Payne, not for one day, not for one minute. There wasn't enough gap in time for me to have had him all to myself.

"No, I mean really," she said. "When will she be gone?"

"I told you, she'll fuck up and leave. She'll fuck herself with her drinking."

"You don't know that. It could take years. Why don't you just throw her out? You don't have any legal obligations."

"She could cause trouble, believe me. I can't explain. You don't want to know. But I'll take care of it. She'll be gone one way or another."

I pressed the back of my head against the wall, trying to use pain to block what was forming in my mind. He knew I would never leave him. That was one way I'd never go. I could only guess what he meant by another. He was either bullshitting the girl, keeping up his act, or he had a plan. I felt a chill. I thought of how easy Brenda just stopped breathing and how easy Hank slipped away. I realized I had all that murder in me, and Payne wasn't much different.

"I don't understand what you're waiting for. She could almost be your mother." She stopped talking and I pictured her prim freckled face stuck up at his. "The woman purposely burned you," she said.

I felt the black truth of it.

"Look, in a short time I can sell the property and the shop. We'll have everything we want, like I told you. Forever. It's too soon right now."

"I don't care about money. I only want you, Payne. I want to get married like you promised."

"I'm not going to talk about this any more. You're ruining our time together. You'll never understand—and I don't want you to bring up that burn again."

He was wrong. She would understand. I was going to fix it so she would understand everything. Show her he could never be trusted, he lacked all feelings. She'd get over him. I didn't care what happened to me. I deserved whatever I got. I just wanted to show him how it felt to be used.

The bed creaked and clothes started to rustle and zip again. I wanted to leap out and tell her the truth right then, but it wasn't the way. I stayed down behind the chair, tried to keep the blood from burning through my veins. I breathed through my mouth to keep quiet. I wanted to get him alone.

I listened to the smoothing of sheets and plumping of pillows, then the clomp of his boots and her bouncing steps through the hall. They stopped.

"Will you call me tonight before I go to bed?" she asked him.

"We'll see," he said.

The fucking asshole—I started rolling through the nights in my mind, trying to think if he made any phone calls in another room. I hadn't noticed. All this time I hadn't thought to check on the son of a bitch.

The door closed and locked. Radar's toenails clicked back into the bedroom. I stayed behind the chair to be safe—in case they'd forgot something—till Radar walked right up and licked my cheek. He knew what was going on.

"Good boy," I said, "You love me dontcha, boy." I rubbed him under his chin and kissed his long velvet nose. He hadn't given me away. He was loyal. I couldn't think about leaving him.

I grabbed the gun and straightened up and walked over to the bed. I got back down on my knees and reached under and pulled out the smooth box. I needed more ammo to give Payne something to remember for the rest of his life. I wanted to fire some shots, do some damage around the shop. I wasn't sure what else. I dropped the bullets in my pocket. I felt the weight of the gun in both hands. It gave me something solid to hold onto.

twenty-two

I'D STOPPED AND GOT A SIX-PACK AND WAS DOWN-ing the third beer when I pulled into the lot at the new store. The last employee was driving off. I didn't want to wait till Payne got home. The chances of anybody hearing shots were much less at the shop. He'd still be finishing up and I could have him all to myself.

His car was pulled up to the building and I parked jam against it, crimping his bumper, so he couldn't walk out on me. He was gonna hear every word I had to say.

I unlocked the door and opened it. Payne was up front scooping change out of the register. I could hear he still had the steamer to turn off. He always left it till he made his last check. Maybe it was some kind of superstition.

He had the radio on, playing country. I passed the dry

cleaning machine and saw the back of his head up at the counter. His soft white neck almost glowed, even from that distance, but I stopped looking at it. I was done with him. All that was done. He heard my footsteps and turned around quick.

He hollered, "Sherri, what are you doing here?"

I just kept walking. He watched me.

"What's the matter?"

He was standing there holding a half-filled roll of quarters, poking his thumb into it like he was massaging a twat. I didn't say anything until I got right up to his face.

"You gonna fuck those quarters?"

"Hey, what's the matter with you?" He plunked the roll down on the counter and some of the quarters flew out and landed on the floor. One rolled around on the counter like a top and I couldn't take my eyes off it.

I smacked it down with my hand. I'm free of him, I told myself. I raised my eyes slow to his face.

"So what's the matter? You're drunk, aren't you?"

"No, but you'll wish I was."

"Yeah, sure. What's your problem then?" He looked down and started repacking the quarters, all back to business.

"Got some come in your pocket, Payne?" I said. I tried to reach into his side pocket and pull it out, but he grabbed my wrist and held on. "What's wrong with you?"

"You're nothing but fuckin fooey over hooey," I screamed. I felt everything come rushing into my head. "I know about all your lies," I screamed. "I saw you, I saw you with her. The redhead. I watched you."

"What are you saying? You're completely nuts."

"I saw you."

"Katie—the girl with the red hair—is an employee.

That's all. Nothing to me. I don't know what you mean. What are you doing? Trying to make trouble?"

"I know she's nothing to you. Just like me."

"You're my wife."

"Is that a joke? I've been wantin to ask you if that's a joke. What was that stupid fuckin ceremony on the beach for anyway?"

"I'm not going to listen to any more of this crap. Go home and sleep it off."

I just stood there watching, waiting for his answer while he pushed the rest of the quarters into a pile and knocked them off the edge of the counter into his hand. He dropped them and the partial roll into his pocket, slammed the drawer, and snapped off the radio. He grabbed the bank pouch with the rest of the money and walked fast to the back. The son of a bitch still wanted to keep up the game.

I stood there a few seconds, then followed him back slow. The lights in front were going off one by one as I walked. He was trying to move me on out. He opened the door of the boiler room, put the light on in there, and cut the steamer. I could see vapor rising out the door. There was just enough glow to make my way to the back. I stopped in the shadows of the big machines and opened my purse and got the gun. I figured I'd catch his attention that way.

"Let's go, let's get out of here," he yelled up to me. Then everything was quiet. He hadn't even made his last check.

"I'm not done talkin," I yelled back. My voice was louder and stronger than I would've thought.

"Let's go. Come on."

I didn't move.

He left the boiler room light on and opened the back door, stepped out, and closed it. He was just going to leave me in there and go home—or somewhere else. The door

closed and I could feel a flat smile sitting on my face. I'd
foxed him. I heard the door open again and I listened to
his quick footsteps coming back toward the machines. I
had the gun out, holding it down by my side in the dark. I
was leaning casual-like on the reclaimer but I felt the hot
wires burning along the sides of my skull.

"Sherri," he called. I could hear the anger. He came
around the side of the reclaimer. He had the key still sticking out to put in the ignition. "What do you think you're
doing?"

I looked at his fucking baby face in the glow. Those lips
were like a brat kid's, pouting. It made me want to bash
them in, but I kept the gun down.

"You've been goddamned fuckin lying to me for
months." I stared at those lips waiting to see what other lie
would come out, but he stayed quiet. "I was at the house
today. I was in the bedroom—behind the chair—the whole
time you were fuckin the girl."

I heard the keys hit the floor when they fell out of his
hand. He didn't bend down to pick em up.

"Okay. Okay. I was. So what? You have your pastimes—
your booze. The guys you hang out with at the bar."

"Give me a fuckin break. I did everything for you, moth-
erfucker. I almost completely quit drinkin—for you. I lived
for you. I fuckin killed a human being for you."

I just kept spittin the truth in front of him. "I fixed it so
we could be together. So Brenda couldn't hurt you anymore."

I looked at his face hard. "I bet she never did nothin to
you—except what you asked for."

"She did plenty. You know it. And you saved me from
her. You set me free. I'm sick of hearing about it. We're
together, aren't we? I married you, didn't I? I'm paid up."

"Married me, shit. Paid up? Fuckin paid up?"

He shifted his weight onto his left foot and put his fist on his hip. He looked like a whining little kid. "Yeah, paid up. I fixed everything for you too. Took care of you."

"I never needed your money or things."

"No? Besides that. I took care of Brian."

"Brian?"

"Yeah. Your old boyfriend. Remember him?"

I couldn't think. What did he know about Brian? "He wasn't my boyfriend—ever. I made a mistake. I would never've gone to him if you didn't throw me out."

"It doesn't matter. I got rid of him."

"What do you mean?"

"He called me up on your behalf—for the second time—to tell me how much you loved me and how I better be taking good care of you—or else he'd tip off the police on property he thought I'd inherited. He said he owed me some trouble for old times' sake. The cocky bastard always hated me. But your ass would have been caught too."

"What property?"

"There isn't any. You know that. I don't know what he was talking about, but I knew he wanted to draw more attention to my assets and give me a motive."

"A motive? Oh. So what did you say?"

"I explained that he was mistaken about the property and told him you and I were doing great. I said, 'Yeah, man. Sherri's the love of my life and always will be.'"

His eyes looked into mine. "I meant it too, baby. I apologized for getting him into trouble all those years ago. I told him I'd changed—told him we were getting married and everything was great. He said he would be looking for the announcement in the church bulletin."

"Our Catholic wedding."

"Yeah. I thought it would be a good idea to show him how serious I was. He'd already called once while you were with him. Said he had some information on me and I better leave you alone. He didn't say you were there, but it was obvious. He said he'd been checking stuff out since he heard about my mother's death."

Payne frowned. "At first I thought you told him something—were setting me up," he said. "The police had already come asking more questions. I think Brian was trying a little blackmail game on a hunch. He didn't know he had so much to lose."

"I never told him nothing, Payne. I only wanted you back, not to hurt you."

"That's what I told him—that we loved each other. I just wanted you back, wanted to marry you. It was true. I wanted you with me—I wanted to be safe again with you. When you came back a few days later I thought he'd told you what I said."

"He didn't tell me anything."

"Anyway, there was no reason to go through with the big wedding. I knew I couldn't trust him. I called him up and invited him for breakfast on the beach—to see for himself how good you and I were together. Said we'd make it a day—"

"You never asked me to go for breakfast on the beach." I could feel the sweat trickling down between my tits.

Payne's mouth had a hint of a smile. "Not for breakfast. Not our beach."

"What?" I asked. "What are you fuckin sayin?"

"I got up while you were still asleep. I told the smart-ass you were off getting the food and you'd be there soon. Then I asked him to give me a surfing lesson." Payne shot me his smug look. "I gave him one instead."

"What do you mean?" I said. My brain was packed with smog.

"It was early, nobody was around. I figured I'd get my

chance. I did. I gave him a bonk on the noggin with his own surfboard. I wish you could have seen it. He never even caught a wave."

"You just fuckin killed him like that?"

"Nope. Actually he drowned—you know how it works. I held him down a few minutes and he did it all by himself. I pushed him out past the waves and left him with his ankle in the bungie cord. He made a sort of anchor for the surfboard, just bumping along."

My throat was tight. A rock was sitting on my chest. I wanted to scream and claw at my face. I'd started it all by killing Brenda. I stood there frozen.

"Nobody saw you?"

"Nope. I swam about a mile up the beach and left. Nobody came by while I was anywhere around. It was probably hours before they found him—you know how those old people walk with their heads down. I went home and woke you and took you off to Key West."

I was stunned. What I thought was my wonderful weekend was a black cover over Brian's murder. "You didn't need to kill him. He couldn't hurt you. I would've confessed before I let you take the blame."

"I was still the accessory. Besides—I told you—Brian's death was accidental. I read about it the next day in the *Herald*. I was afraid to let you see it. But now you need to know all I've done for us."

He put his hand in his pocket, jangled the quarters.

"Brian was too old for surfing. It could have happened by itself—just like my mother's death."

Brian and Brenda, I thought. It made prickles on my scalp. I pictured them both out there together, skin peeling off, floating under the surface. I thought of my father and Hank too. They were all together somehow.

Payne's lips puckered and he reached out and twisted a piece of my hair. He'd enjoyed telling me.

"So, you see, my dear, I saved your ass."

"Your own," I said. My throat was stiff. I felt how heavy the gun was down at my side.

"That too. I saved it for you."

"You did, huh?" I felt the explosions in my brain closing my eyes to slits. "For me and your little girlfriend."

"No, I'm finished with her. She just pushed her way back into my life. I never intended to keep that going. It'll be just us again. I promise." He reached out to put his hand behind my neck.

I stepped back, pulled up the gun with both hands and pointed it at his chest. It took him a second to catch the glint. I watched him suck air and stiffen up. I heard the thud when the money pouch slid out from under his arm and hit the floor.

"Oh, yeah," I said. "And what was that plan you mentioned, for gettin rid of me?"

"Sherri, take it easy. You're wrong. I was just shutting her up—until I could figure how to break up with her—so she wouldn't make a fuss. So you and I could be together again, like we're supposed to be, just the two of us."

I didn't know if he was telling the truth or a lie. It didn't matter at all. It even seemed worse if he was telling the truth. It showed he couldn't care about anybody, ever. I just kept holding the gun straight at his heart, feeling the power of it.

He was breathing hard. "What the fuck? What are you doing with that?"

"I'm playin with it, strokin it. It's hard and ready. It works good. Remember how you worked me with it? Just like you worked me with your cock."

I looked at his baby face in the shadow and motioned with the gun toward his face. "Did you use this on your mom, too?"

"You're insane. Give it to me."

"I bet you did. I bet you got it specially to use on her."

He didn't answer. It all made me sick. I saw him standing there looking as pretty and clean as always. His soft tan pants were perfectly creased. I could see where his balls rested alongside the seam. The place where it all started.

"Give me the gun, Sherri. Give it to me so we can go home. Be together. Make love. Make it good again."

"Fuck," I said. "We can't make it good. There's no good. It was all in my imagination. You never wanted me except to use me."

"Come on. That's not true. You made your own choice."

"I didn't make a choice. I didn't have the truth to choose from. You made me do everything with your lies." It struck me that he could've planned it all along—for either the girl or me to get him out. He just didn't get that far. Then again, maybe I was nuts. I knew I'd never find out the whole truth. It didn't even matter.

"We're good for each other. You know it. Come on, babe."

He'll never quit, I thought. Nothing can get to him. He just keeps spreading his germs.

I tilted my head toward the dry cleaning machine. "Get in there."

He stood squinting at me.

"I mean it. Get in the machine." I kept the gun steady. "I mean it."

He walked to the machine and unlatched the round door and turned to me. He was still looking like we were playing some game, not sweating or nervous that I could tell.

"Let's go home," he said. "Everything's all right. You've just had a few too many. You're just not realizing how good you've got it. I love you."

He managed to sound like he meant it—more than usual. I couldn't stand it. "I've had a few too many of your lies, fuck yes."

I squeezed a shot off into the ceiling and chunks of cement came down like hail, hitting the floor and bouncing around. I put another one into the concrete by his left foot. It sprayed us both with gravel and tore a good size hole. I held the gun out straight at his chest again and cocked it, for effect. He knew how fast it worked cocked. His face froze, but he lifted one leg and stepped backwards into the machine and hunched down and pulled in the other leg. He sat back and squeezed his shoulders through. I thought how graceful he did it, but I didn't care. He was looking at me from the round black hole. It was like a picture.

"C'mon baby," he said. "We're two of a kind. We're together. We'll always be."

When I heard those words, I was done thinking. I couldn't stand it, the same fucking two words I heard him say to her. I started shouting right into his face. "Liar, liar, fuckin, motherfuckin liar." My voice sounded like somebody else's, it was so hoarse and low. "I thought you were the most goddamn wonderful person I ever knew. I thought I was goddamn lucky you wanted me. I just had to stop her from hurtin you—you poor fuckin sweet lamb."

I slammed the metal door and he started screaming. I could tell by his mouth he was giving all his volume, but it was a tiny voice inside the machine. I flipped the handle down and it was locked. I punched the button that put a second lock on so it couldn't be opened from the outside either, until the cycle was complete. His face was mashed against the little round glass. He was hammering with his fists.

I sat down in front of the door and put the gun on my lap. I could look right into his wild eyes and hear his hollow screams and feel numb. Once I started the flow I knew it wouldn't take long for the fumes or the fluid to quiet him down. I wanted to let him have his little scream first. Maybe he was praying. He needed some time to feel sorry for his sins.

I thought about the cat piss that contaminated everything. His stench would do the same. Somebody would have to change it. Not me.

I put my hand out and drew on the glass with my finger. His eyes. His eyebrows. He was staring straight at me screaming in this little voice. He sounded like a fucking sheep. I traced down the nose to his lips. Rooster, pullet, hen. Rooster, pullet, hen. Touch the forehead—rooster. Nose—pullet. Chin—hen. It was a kids' game old Darrell used to play when he wasn't on top of me. Funny thing to think about then.

Darrell would keep repeating it till it made me crazy. Then he'd stop at the nose. "What'd I say this was?" he'd ask. I knew what was coming and I hated it, but he'd keep asking until I had to say it. "Pull-it." Then he'd give a burning pinch with those fingers on my nose. Payne's nose was squashed on the glass. It wasn't burning yet. He kept screaming.

I put my hand flat to cover his lips. He was still screaming. He got up then and I couldn't see him. He started kicking the door. That was it. I stood and punched the buttons to make the fluid flow. The machine started its roll and the screaming stopped. I couldn't see but I knew it was flipping him up the sides and dropping him down the middle.

It was a powerful machine and it was clunking, working hard. His shoes were bumping the sides, or maybe it was his head. I pictured his mouth open and the powerful cleaning fluid filling his mouth, lungs, stomach—pooling in his ears, penetrating into his skin, burning through the tiny pipe of his cock, tearing its way like a knife up his asshole. He would soon be cleaner than any human ever got. His stench would be filtered and dumped with the toxic waste.

"I loved you," I said. It was just a whisper in the empty building.

I picked up the gun and walked back to the door. The extra bullets clicked in my pocket. I didn't need them. I turned out the lights and locked. I don't know why. It didn't matter. I just thought I'd go home. Go to sleep in the rose sheets. Nothing left mattered.

Radar was wagging his furry butt right inside the door when I opened it, and I squatted down and let him lick my face. How could I have forgotten about him? He still loved me.

My hands were almost numb. I had to think how to work my fingers. I smoothed the shiny fur on his head and held it. The skin moved back a little so I could see the clean whites at the tops of his eyes, stark against the black edges of his lids. He looked at me, chin up, not blinking. I pressed my face against his cheek. He loved me. He was the only one. I had to take care of him.

He followed me into the kitchen and I set down my purse with the gun in it and picked up his plastic bowl. He always got dry food with one egg. I opened the refrigerator and there were six eggs in the door. I picked out two at a

time and put them all on the counter. I got his sack of dry
food from under the sink. His head followed the food and
he watched me while I filled the bowl all the way to the rim
and put the sack away. Then I cracked the eggs against the
side of the plastic and opened them slow not to break a
yolk and dropped each one gentle on the top of the food,
until I had six shiny orange eyes that shimmered at me
when I set the bowl down. Radar's head followed the bowl
and he went to licking at the closest yolk. He was happy. At
least I could make somebody happy. I patted his head and
fingered his ears.

I went to the cabinet to get the bottle Payne called cooking sherry. It was just goddamned wine like all the rest. I
never drank even a sip since he accused me of it. I could
still hear his voice. "The wine level was above the label yesterday. Now it's down here at the Gallo."

I'd said I was the only "cookin' Sherri" I knew anything
about. I said, "I'm cookin right now." I tried to get my body
against his and give him a kiss, but he held stiff and smelled
at my breath. Didn't even smile. As if gulping an inch and
a half of wine would've done me some good. "If I'd have
drunk on it, that bottle would be in the trash bin by now,"
I told him.

That was a lifetime ago.

I sat down on the tile next to Radar and took a hit off the
wine and watched him lick at his last egg. He hadn't
touched the hard food yet. He licked gentle at the yolk and
it wobbled under his tongue for a few seconds until the
thin skin broke and it lost its shape and spread down into
the kibble. What a funny word. Payne always used it. I was
still hearing his fucking words. Fucking kibble.

I sat there sucking on the warm sherry and waited for
Radar till he finished crunching his last piece. It took him

a long time and I polished off the wine, but I wasn't feeling it. I was just feeling empty.

I stood and dropped the bottle in the trash. Radar got up and lapped some water from his dish and walked on over to the glass doors. He dropped his old bones and let out that sigh he always made when he plopped down. I watched his side move in and out with his calm breathing. He was content looking out toward the ocean, but from his level he could probably only see sand.

I got the gun from my purse and cocked it for a fast squeeze. I walked over to him and squatted down.

"Love you, buddy," I said. I stroked down the shiny hair on the back of his neck.

He just kept looking at the sand. His soft pink tongue was hanging out a little, vibrating on the edges with his breath. He was calm. I didn't touch him. I put the gun behind the crown of his head so I could be sure to finish it instantly. I couldn't let him feel anything. He didn't look around. It was the toughest thing I ever did. I pulled the trigger.

The force of the shot jerked my hands and knocked my ass back on the floor. When I looked up, the glass in the door had turned to white crystals. I'd blown a gaping hole, but the glass hung frozen like a wall of cracked ice. Then it crashed in a heap and sprayed bits in all directions. Radar leaped up and started to bark, frantic and wild.

I swallowed and gaped at him, not seeing any blood. I'd missed. Bad aim must've run in the family. I didn't know what to do, but I couldn't try it again.

He was still barking crazy at the smashed door. "Quiet, lover," I said. "It's okay." I took his snout in my hands to calm him and kissed the white hair above his nose. He finally settled down. I went to the cabinet and pulled out the twenty-five pound sack of dog food and ripped it open down the side. I got a bucket from under the sink and filled it with water. I hoped somebody would find him before everything was gone. He looked at me wide-eyed, breathing heavy, but spared from knowing that I'd tried to kill him.

I turned around and walked into the bedroom and he followed and laid down on the rug. I took off all my clothes and sat on the bed Indian style. I put the gun, cold and heavy, on my thigh. It was pointed towards me, towards my pussy exactly. I looked at the long dark roots grown in, the blond left only on the tips. It had taken a long time to grow out. Payne liked it dark. So he'd said.

I wanted to feel sorry for all the killing, but I couldn't. I sat there forever, but I couldn't feel nothing.

I picked up the gun and saw the lines from it indented on my skin. I stroked the cold metal, pushed the release and clicked out the cylinder. Three shots left. That's how I wanted it—fifty-fifty. Leave it all to fate. I turned the cylinder around, around, around, and clicked it back into the gun without looking. I lowered it, slid it inside me, underneath the black roots. I tensed the muscle in my finger and squeezed on the trigger. A little, a little more. I could feel when there was only one squeeze left. I wondered if Radar would lick my blood as it drained. Take the nourishment if he needed it. I thought, wherever I'm going, it can't be fucking far enough. I squeezed.

epilogue

I SIT UP IN BED AND LOOK OUT MY APARTMENT window. I can only see the dirty brick side of the next building, but the gray light tells me it's another cold, shitty day in Baltimore. It'll stay that way. One thing about Baltimore—you know where you stand.

I get up and put on the one pair of jeans I brought with me and the old sweater. Except for my little driftwood lamp and Radar, I left everything else. I hoped the police would think somebody got me too, and the dog ran off through the shattered door. Fat chance, but none of the stuff was mine anyway. Never was.

I drag on the heavy coat I bought from the Salvation Army store with money from the cash register. I'd gone back and emptied the bank pouch and dropped it on the floor to make it look like robbery. It was $800, so I had enough money for the coat, and rent, and food for a couple weeks.

I packed the gun and money and a few things in my old suitcase. Radar and me drove over to Dixie Highway and then north a ways until we fit in natural with the scenery. I stuck out my thumb and got us both a ride. I would've been out of Florida faster alone, but I couldn't leave him. There were enough men willing to let a collie hop in the back seat if they could gander at my packed bikini top up front.

Now I have a job dancing on "The Block." It's easy walking distance from my Charles Street apartment. A raunchy place, but it's cheap and they let me have the dog. I'm close to the Inner Harbor. Walked there once. It gave me nightmares about Brenda and Brian—both of them bloated, gliding after me. I might as well have done in Brian too. It was all my fault. I don't know how I could've been so wrong.

I put Radar on his leash and open the door and tramp down the hollow wood stairs, out into the cold. We walk to the newsstand a few blocks away where they sell the *Miami Herald.*

Old Ben behind the counter looks up and grins.

"Morning, Cher," he says.

I've dyed my hair black and shortened my name to go with the look.

"Mornin. Got a winner for me this mornin?" I'm really looking to see if there's any news on Payne's murder, but I told Ben I bet the horses at Gulfstream, and the *Herald* is where I check the winner and pick my next horse.

I put my change on the counter, take my paper, and page to the end of the sports section. I look at it, shake my head.

"Nope. No winner for me," I say. "Good thing. I wouldn't know how to handle it if I had a streak of luck."

"Well, there's always tomorrow," he says.

"Yeah. Except on Sunday."

"Huh?"

"The horses don't run on Mondays."

He chuckles and nods. I fold the paper and tuck it under my arm. Radar and me hoof it back through the slush.

When I get home I take a cup of coffee, pour some Jack in it, and sit down to read the news. I missed a couple weeks in the beginning, before I figured how to buy a Miami paper without being suspicious. I saw a followup article later about Payne's murder being drug-related. I guess they always think that in Miami. My name wasn't mentioned, so I couldn't tell if they were after me. I keep checking. I know it's not over.

I look at an ad for a dry cleaners, wonder if it's the old Purity with a new name. I slide my finger down the classifieds. There's a "help wanted, experienced pressers," another one "experienced help." That's me. But I'm done with cleaning. I picture the sign in the window luring me inside on the first day, and I know I'll take that trip again—in my nightmares.

I glance over at the mattress. The gun is wedged between it and the box spring. It comforts me to touch the hard metal when I go to sleep. I keep one bullet loaded—threw the rest away. No messing with the pussy. Just one lined up for when they come to take me in. When I see em through the peephole, I'll get the gun and go down on my knees for one last blow job. I'll wedge my arms so I can't miss.

Till then I've got a bottle, Radar, and my old trade. There's Alwyn—a tall Jamaican—one floor up. He has dreads and good dope, and a space between his front bottom teeth where I like to poke my tongue—leave the pain for a while. Payne. It's still the same.

I wonder what Payne had in his mind, and I feel guilty about killing Brenda. But none of it matters. I'll pay up. That's the way things go.

I look back out the window through streaks of wet grime. The sky is still gray, and water drips off the icy gutter. Let that red sun shine down on Miami, like always, and make the blue eyes sparkle with promises for somebody else. Ain't no sunshine in Baltimore. The sky's solid and cold, like a heart that's stopped.